The Robbery at Boulder Halt

The four tough Lawson boys rode into Boulder Halt, desperate to raise cash to save brother number five, in jail in Austin. With six-guns blazing, they storm Frank Warren's bank and burst out with a gunny-sack of cash – but the price is high. Tom Lawson is gunned down by Marshal Nat Kimball, young Buck Lawson is taken by Deputy Jim Folsom and, inside the bank, Frank Warren's daughter takes two bullets in the chest.

Through a wind-torn night, Owen and Adam Lawson make it out of town with the cash, then go their separate ways. Adam follows the railroad to Austin; Owen returns to Boulder Halt without his beard and, wearing Adam's hat, is determined to rescue Buck.

What transpires in that tough border town is as surprising as it is exciting. Owen Lawson battles to free his brother, and finally negotiates a risky deal that promises to ensure justice and their safety. Only a fool would believe such a deal will be honoured!

The Robbery at Boulder Halt

MATT LAIDLAW

A Black Horse Western

ROBERT HALE · LONDON

ISBN 0 7090 6948 0

Robert Hale Limited
Clerkenwell House
Clerkenwell Green
London EC1R 0HT

Typeset by
Derek Doyle & Associates, Liverpool.
Printed and bound in Great Britain by
Antony Rowe Limited, Wiltshire.

Chapter One

There was sweat on his face and on his hands and he cursed softly as the rifle he was loading with bright brass shells slipped, the muzzle poking into the dirt between his boots. He looked up to see Owen watching him from the shadows under the wet trees and at once flashed a grin that split his beardless face and brought a defiant glint to his blue eyes.

'I guess you was like this, before your first bank job,' he said shakily. 'All fingers and thumbs, mouth as sour as a desert water-hole?'

'You'll be fine,' Owen Lawson said, 'soon's we ride into town.'

He slipped the thin Bowie knife he had been using on his fingernails into his right boot, climbed to his feet and walked past the boy crouched by the flickering fire. As the moon drifted across a fleeting gap between monstrous

5

clouds, his long shadow followed him in an arc across the shine of the wet leaves as he crossed to the tethered horses under the trees where Adam was talking with Tom.

'The kid's findin' it tough,' he said, and saw the two exchange glances. Then tall, rawboned Adam Lawson pulled a cinch tight with a snap and shrugged.

'There ain't no easy way of snatchin' that much money.'

'Always supposin' there's as much loot there as you say there is,' Tom Lawson said. His horse was saddled, ready, the man as lean and angular as his twin brother and with the same obstinate look on his handsome, bearded face that was a direct challenge to Owen.

Owen Lawson nodded, his back suddenly tight, his breathing shallow.

'Yeah, I figured as much. You two are still arguing about how much goddamn cash we stand to gain instead of—'

'It's got to be worth it,' Tom said stubbornly. He straightened, squaring his bony shoulders, his frame matching that of the rangy sorrel horse. 'Ain't no use—'

'For Christ's sake!' Owen Lawson said. 'If there ain't enough cash in that safe then we ride to the next town, do it again. And again, and again, for as long as it takes.'

'But not too long,' Tom said.

'Every time,' Adam said, his eyes bleak, 'the risks'll get higher, and all for—'

Owen stepped forward, and for an instant it seemed that he would hit his tall, lean brother. Then, moving with deceptive speed, Tom came away from the sorrel and Owen was hemmed in, his fist bunched, his lips white with anger. He took a breath; the moment passed. 'We're doing this for Ike,' he said, his eyes locked on Adam's face, his will a blazing force lighting his blue eyes. 'What's at stake here is your brother's life.'

'That's what was at stake,' Adam said. 'What's at stake as soon as we walk into that bank is the lives of Ike Lawson's four younger brothers.' His gaze was steady, his high cheekboned face registering deep concern. 'You think Ma could accept that? Would allow you to take that awful risk?'

'For God's sake!' Owen said. 'You're putting me in one hell of a cleft stick, Adam. Ike is Ma's first-born. A grown man, sure, but still the boy she loves more than life itself. With him facing the hangman's noose in Austin jail that makes me senior, makes the family my responsibility. Ma's looking to me to bring him home, not those four owlhoot pards Ike's got setting there in Austin looking for ways to bust him out. Us, not them – and you know why. So we do it, and how it's done. . . .' He paused, rubbed his hands on his thighs, biting back the words "doesn't matter" because they suggested sentiments at odds with those of a man who had just voiced his responsibility for the family's safety.

'How it's done,' he said quietly, 'is not for Ma to know.'

'Unless it goes wrong,' Adam said.

'Right now,' Owen Lawson said, 'things are about as wrong as they can get. So forget what Ike is, or what he's done. He's Lawson, and he's kin. I figure that's worth any risk, don't you?'

'Yeah, dammit, he's a Lawson, but—'

'No buts. And you know Tom's right. We can't take too long over this. In Austin, lawyers cost money. Your brother'll hang for murder 'less we produce one, and fast. So we get cash, and when we've got it, one of of us goes for a long ride in one hell of a hurry.'

'Which is exactly why I was pointin' out the risks,' Adam said. 'Ain't no sense gettin' hold of a pile of cash money, if every damn one of us is dead.'

'All right,' Owen said. 'So we take one step at a time.'

'If you fellers argue much longer, Ike'll be dead and buried.'

The boy had moved away from the fire, the Winchester now gleaming, his strong hands firm on the oiled weapon. There was still the sheen of

8

sweat on his young face, but now there was a strange light in his eyes. Unnaturally wide, they caught the high cold light of dawn filtering through the trees where he stood and became luminous. He was a trapped animal, his eyes the window to a soul in which common sense and the raw courage of youth were being swamped by panic. For an instant, that panic threatened to spread in waves over the three men who had been startled by his silent approach. Then the boy turned his head. A twig crackled underfoot as he came closer. The reflected light in his blue eyes winked out, the illusion abruptly dispelled.

'Time we was gone,' he said, and jerked a thumb at the bleak dawn skies.

'He's right,' Owen said gruffly, and moved to let his hand rest lightly on the boy's shoulder. 'So let's go over it one more time—'

'Jesus!' Adam Lawson breathed disgustedly, then slid his eyes away from Owen's furious glance.

'I ride in first,' Owen said. 'You three keep a check on the time, follow so's you're riding into town from the west as the bank opens on the stroke of nine. We all know where the marshal'll be. He takes cash to the bank every day at that same time. So just watch for me. If there's trouble, you'll see me mount up, ride out the east side of town. If all's well, I'll cross the street and go into the bank.'

'Robbin' a bank is all trouble,' Adam said. 'A

man can spend twelve months makin' plans, see every goddamn one of them blown away when—'

'Follow me into the bank as fast as you can,' Owen said. 'Buck, when we're inside, you watch the horses.'

'Sure,' Buck Lawson said. He hefted the Winchester and grinned. 'Anyone makes a move, I'll—'

'That deputy comes out of the jail, you fire a shot into the air then get the hell out of town. Same thing goes if you hear shooting from inside the bank. Don't wait around. Don't take chances. Mount up, get the hell out of there and head for home.'

The wind sighed. Overhead, branches rustled. Heavy drops spattered the ground. The rain had cleared, but the skies were lowering. A day to match the grimness of what they were planning, Owen Lawson reflected, and for an instant his hand tightened on his youngest brother's shoulder.

Then, decisively, he pushed him away.

'All clear?'

They nodded. Adam Lawson. Then Tom Lawson. Last of all but the most eagerly, the eighteen-year-old boy, Buck Lawson, who was fighting a plucky battle against fear.

'All right,' said Owen Lawson. 'Let's get this over with.'

Chapter Two

Caught and lifted by the wind, a sheet of rain swept horizontally across Boulder Halt's main street. It rattled across the rusting trash cans in the alley, added its slickness to the shiny timbers of the plankwalk fronting the blind windows of the mercantile, spattered the pools and greasy mud under the empty hitch-rail as the gust swirled and died.

On the other side of the street, the door of the jail rattled, then banged open. Yellow lamplight flooding from the opening was a warm contrast to the wet, grey morning. A big man reluctantly emerged, a badge glittering on the front of his mackinaw. He turned, spoke briefly to the tall, lean man framed in the doorway. Then he threw a swift glance up and down the street, settled his Stetson firmly on his long black hair and tugged his coat collar up around his ears. Behind him, the door slammed to.

Carrying a small linen sack, he started along the plankwalk, his shoulder tight up against the fronts of the buildings as the wind moaned.

From a doorway directly opposite the bank, Owen Lawson drew deeply on the cigarette in his cupped hand and watched the town marshal dispassionately. He saw him walk as far as the Land Office, step down from the plankwalk, heard the muttered curse as booted feet sank to the ankles in mud, watched him angle across the street, head ducked against the driving rain. The lawman looked up once, splashed past the rail where Owen's horse stood with drooping head, pushed open the bank's heavy door and stepped inside.

One man. The bank's first customer. And the street was empty.

To the left of the door, and higher up, the bank's big barred window was a bright square of light. Through it, Owen could see the heavy timepiece on the back wall. That clock, he knew, was sited directly above the big iron safe.

Almost nine o'clock.

If the clock was right.

Patiently, Owen dragged the battered turnip watch from his pocket, checked the time, snapped it shut and put it away.

He knew Tom and Adam would be doing the same, at frequent intervals.

And with a noticeable quickening of his pulse he turned his head to look east, his eyes moving across the shabby hotel that stood alongside the bank, on in a line across the street to the silent saloon and the tonsorial parlour and beyond them the thinning row of buildings past which he would have been riding if there had been trouble; then back, warily, down the empty street, eyes squinted as he peered through the curtain of drifting rain.

The jail's door was shut. Deputy Jim Folsom would stay inside hugging the pot-bellied stove until the marshal's return. Across from the jail the mercantile with its wide stoop and stacked barrels was now open, but the only sign of movement was the flapping of its sign, the only noise a faint, rusty creaking. Greasy curtains hung in a loop across the windows of Annie's Café, the thin net sticking to the steamed-up glass. The smell of frying steak came and went with the gusts. A cowhand cut across the street, one hand planted on his hat, and disappeared into the runway of Stolt's Livery and Feed.

Owen had counted to fifty, tight nerves drying his mouth, his lips moving soundlessly, when the riders appeared. They crossed the railroad a hundred yards away. Three men, one wearing a glistening yellow slicker, two in long white dusters hanging wet and limp, filthy hems brushing stirrups. They rode at a walk up the centre of the street, their horses splashing mud, the white vapour of their breath caught and torn by the wind.

Decisively, Owen flicked away the cigarette. He swept back his slicker, brushed a hand across his Colt, then stepped out of the doorway. The wind caught the slicker, flapping it as he went across the muddy street at an awkward jog. Without looking up, without making any sign, he was aware of the riders, caught the breathy snorting of their horses, the jingle of bridles.

Then he was across. He touched his horse, the wet leather of the saddle, saw its head lift, its ears flick in recognition. He stepped up on to the side-walk, then immediately moved aside, nodding politely, as the blonde-haired, elegant woman he had seen coming out of the hotel hastened past him, her head ducked against the rain. He caught the scent of her perfume, felt her long dress brush his knee as it was caught by the wind. Then she was gone.

Noisily, Owen Lawson stamped mud off his boots – for stealth had no part in this plan – and went into the bank.

The hiss of the wind and rain was reduced intantly to a soft soughing. Owen's nostrils flared to the warm stink of a coal-oil stove, the rich aroma of hot coffee. As he shook rain from his slicker and flipped it open in the natural move-

14

ment a man would make, one swift glance told him all he needed to know, confirmed everything he had observed in the thirty minutes he had stood in the draughty shadows.

Frank Warren, the bank's owner, was behind the counter with his coat off, arm-bands glittering against the blue and white stripes of the shirt that was strained across his massive chest. A dark-haired girl in a blue cotton dress, face flushed, a lock of hair sweeping to brush her cheek as she attended to the marshal under Warren's watchful gaze. Marshal Nat Kimball, steaming tin cup in his right hand, linen bag flat and empty on the counter before him watched as the cashier counted the taxes, licence fees and sundry fines and payments the marshal had brought along to be deposited.

'Damn weather!' Owen Lawson said softly.

The marshal grunted without turning, his eyes on the pretty cashier's fingers.

Then he stiffened as the muzzle of Owen's .45 bored into the small of his back and the hammer went back with a loud click.

'Seems to me,' Owen went on, his voice still low, steady, 'it ain't at all the kind of weather a man would choose to get buried – if he had a say in his own funeral. You have, Marshal. Just plant both hands flat on the counter, and stay as still as a wooden Injun.'

15

'Have you figured out some way of robbin' this bank,' Kimball said through his teeth, 'with you behind me holdin' that pistol and Frank's big safe up against the back wall?'

The door crashed open. Boots thundered on the board floor. The damp swept in, bringing with it clammy fingers of fear.

'Something just occurred,' Owen Lawson said, 'to solve that problem.'

The girl was motionless, her face as white as bone. Warren's eyes had narrowed. The marshal's head began to turn.

'Face front,' Owen warned.

'No masks, Nat.' These were the first words Frank Warren had uttered. His voice was contemptuous. 'They don't mind being recognized, so they're not local men.'

'But we've been watching for a week, we're here, right now, all four of us, and that's all any of you need to know,' Owen Lawson said. 'So, feller, why don't you just grab your keys, and open up that safe?'

'Over my dead body,' Warren gritted, and suddenly there was the sheen of sweat on his balding scalp.

'No,' Owen said easily. 'Open it, or the girl dies.'

'My daughter.' And now there was deadly menace in the bank-owner's voice.

'In that case,' Owen said, 'you've got one helluva

16

good reason to move fast.'

'Damn you!'

For an instant Warren hung there, poised between the defiance that would come naturally to a man powerful in physique and reputation, and the instinct for survival and the safety of his own flesh and blood. The marshal stood motionless, big hands flat on the counter. The girl, dark eyes enormous, looked beyond Owen Lawson to the tall men in white dusters who had pushed the door shut and moved into the room.

Then Frank Warren stirred. He swung on his heel, his hands dropping to his belt. Keys clinked. He walked to the black safe, with a steady hand inserted a key, twisted it. The lock clicked. The door, hinged on the left, swung open, stopped with its edge up against his chest.

Behind Owen Lawson, a man let his breath go. Boots scraped on the boards.

'Step back,' Owen said. 'Move away from the safe. You and your daughter go stand facing the wall alongside the stove.'

Warren appeared to straighten. His big frame stood square and solid, back to the counter. His left hand had lifted and reached across his body to grasp the edge of the safe door. He would need to step back half a pace to swing the door open and to his left. Then, if he chose to do it, his right hand could reach into the safe.

17

Jesus! Owen thought, that safe's big enough to hold a scattergun.

His six-gun hard up against the marshal's spine, he felt his nerves tighten. In the sudden, aching stillness, it was possible to hear the ragged breathing of nervous men, the faint burbling of the coffee pot on the stove, the ticking of the clock . . . the nervous movements of horses huddled against the hitch-rail in the cold morning rain.

'Dad!'

The girl stepped back from the counter, turned—

'No, Janie!'

Marshal Nat Kimball spoke sharply, leaning across the counter to reach for the girl's wrist. The cup clattered to the floor, splashing coffee. Janie Warren caught herself, seemed about to stop. Then she shook off the marshal's hand, turned decisively.

'Dad, please, give them the money!'

A sudden gust of wind drove rain hard against the windows. The bank's heavy door rattled, the lock clicked and it began to blow open. One of the men swore softly. Someone said, 'Get that damn. . . .'

And Frank Warren made his move.

He stepped back and whipped open the safe door, his hand reaching in to snatch at the six-gun lying on the stacked banknotes as he whirled to face the men intent on robbing his bank.

18

Janie Warren threw herself forward, screaming.

Owen Lawson yelled, 'Don't do it!'

Warren's six-gun roared.

The slug hissed angrily past Owen's ear. He slammed his left forearm hard across the marshal's neck. The blow drove the lawman down across the counter. Owen's right arm came across in a vicious swing. He cracked the barrel of his six-gun along the bone behind the marshal's right ear.

The marshal began to crumple, groaning. Owen pushed the weight of the slack body away from him, spun away from the counter. He saw Warren, backed up against the open safe, jaw jutting, eyes narrowed, six-gun raised and levelled. Then, still screaming, Janie Warren flung herself at her father, her arms locking about his broad shoulders.

Behind Owen Lawson, as the girl sprang to defend her father, a six-gun roared, then another, the twin detonations coming as one.

The girl stiffened. Two black holes appeared in the thin blue cotton of her dress. She arched, whimpering. The black holes below her right shoulder became red and glistening. Her fingers opened, clawing, the nails tearing at Frank Warren's fine striped shirt as she slid to the floor.

Warren's hideaway six-gun clattered to the

floor. He sank alongside his daughter, his big hands swiftly stained with her bright blood as his eyes lifted to stare in sightless horror at the three Lawsons.

Owen Lawson swung to face Adam and Tom, tall figures in filthy white dusters. His mind was numb with horror.

'Get the cash. Move, now!'

Then Buck appeared in the doorway, yellow slicker glistening, face white.

'Owen, that deppity's comin'!'

'Do like I told you. Get the hell out of town!'

As the kid about turned and the big door slammed back against the wall, Owen followed him out into the driving rain. One swift glance told him they were in bad trouble. Some way down the street, the jail's door now gaped wide, yellow lamplight glistening on the wet plankwalk. But that was already some way behind Deputy Jim Folsom who was across the street and heading for the bank with a rifle up across his chest. Behind him, the cowboy was emerging from the livery barn, hatless, but holding a six-gun. And, as Owen watched, two more men came tumbling from Annie's Café, reaching for their pistols.

'Hurry!' he yelled over his shoulder. Then, to Buck, standing frozen alongside his horse with the shiny Winchester, 'Come on, kid, move, ride for your life!'

A shot roared, coming from the east side of town. White splinters flew from the hitch-rail. Horses squealed, lunging in panic. Owen whirled, dropping to a crouch, boots sliding in the yellow mud so that he went to his knees. A man wearing a white apron flapping in the wind was standing outside the saloon, shotgun rammed into his shoulder. Owen snapped a shot. The man yelled, stepped back into the doorway.

When Owen turned back, half falling, Folsom was much closer, Buck atop his plunging bronc and swinging away from the rail. Then Adam and Tom came piling out of the bank, Adam with a fat gunny-sack swinging from his hand.

Breath hissing through his clamped teeth, Owen climbed out of the mud and splashed towards his horse. Tom already had a foot in a stirrup and was swinging over leather, but cursing as his white duster entangled his legs. Adam had unhitched his horse but was struggling to hold the taut reins as the terrified animal backed off, jerking its head high.

Passing close to Buck, Owen whacked the kid's bronc with his fist, drove it away from the plunging mass of tangled horseflesh with the kid holding the Winchester high as he fought to stay in the saddle. Then he'd reached his own horse. A swift flick freed the reins. He grabbed the horn, swung into the saddle.

21

He was wrenching the crazed horse's head around, physically manhandling it away from the bank, when shots began to crackle. The cowboy and the two men from the diner were spaced out along the plankwalk. All three were in range, using their six-guns. Bullets sang around the Lawsons, plucking at clothing, whining into the grey skies. Tom had ripped off his flapping duster; it hung from his saddle and trailed in the mud as he snapped a shot down the street and wheeled away from the rail. Adam was in the saddle, fighting the horse one-handed as he hung on to the gunny-sack.

Then Folsom's rifle began to bark.

Buck's horse went down in a heap, sliding in the greasy mud. The shiny Winchester slapped down, and sank. The kid was stretched out, one leg under the kicking horse, his eyes wild as he struggled to break free.

'Drop your guns! It's over, finished!'

In the doorway of the bank the six-gun glistened in Marshal Nat Kimball's big fist. Blood was running down his neck. He sagged against the door frame. But his long, black hair was a lion's mane, his eyes ablaze.

'Go to hell!' Tom Lawson yelled. He threw down on the marshal. His bullet chipped the woodwork alongside the lawman's bloody neck. Then, tight up against his stirrup, Adam Lawson's horse

22

stepped on his brother's trailing duster. Wrenched sideways, Tom grabbed for the horn. As he did so, Kimball fired. The slug took Tom Lawson just above the belt buckle. He folded, then toppled into the mud.

Owen was clear, in the middle of the street and facing east. Adam went past him, his horse bolting, splashing through the thick mud on a loose rein. For a moment Owen reined back, twisting in the saddle. He took in the men pounding up the sidewalk, six-guns blazing, one of them already leaping into the mud to head for where a weakening Buck fought hopelessly against the weight of his dead horse. Further back, Jim Folsom was down on one knee taking deliberate aim. The badge flashed on big Nat Kimball's chest as he came away from the bank on unsteady legs, his fierce gaze fixed on Owen.

'Leave 'em, Owen!'

Over the rattle of gunfire, Adam's voice trailed back to him. He saw the 'puncher reach Buck, bend to hold a pistol to the kid's head; saw Kimball step stiffly down off the sidewalk, look once at Tom Lawson, then look straight at Owen and shake his head.

Numbly, Owen Lawson wheeled his horse away from the bank, used his spurs to urge the excited horse into a lunging gallop. Wet mud was flying as Adam raced away from him, gunny-sack clutched in one hand. Owen was aware of the roar of the shotgun as he raced past the saloon, felt the wind of the lead shot.

Then he was hammering out of town and, as the crackle of gunfire faded and died, the loudest sound on that bleak morning was the mocking howl of the wind in his ears.

Chapter Three

The rain was in their faces, ice-cold needles driven by the wind, blinding the horses so that Owen and Adam were forced to use their spurs to drive them hard up the long slopes that led north. They pushed on for half an hour, and in that time the wind strengthened but did nothing to sweep away the swollen clouds or diminish the power of the beating rain. Worn deep by horses and cattle, the trail became a churning yellow river. With coats torn back by the wind, both men were soaked to the skin.

But through it all, Adam Lawson kept his hold on the heavy gunny-sack.

Riding in his brother's wake, Owen watched that sack, willing Adam to hang on to it as it bounced heavy against the saddle or was caught by the wind to be lifted high and almost wrenched from the rider's grasp. One minute, too, he was

25

cursing it and wishing it gone, for the brutal and unlawful way it had been taken had led to the most awful tragedy. Then those feelings were washed away by a powerful wave of a different kind of emotion, and he was thanking God for the hope it could give to a man who had nothing to look forward to but the hangman's noose.

And so it was the contents of that sack, and what they meant to the elders of their family – brother and mother – that gave them the will to keep boring onward into the raging teeth of the storm.

But willpower alone was not enough.

Owen Lawson looked over his shoulder.

Behind him, the trail sloped away into an indistinct distance across which the rain swept horizontally in curtains of grey. Through those ragged curtains, nothing could be distinguished. Somewhere, there was the town of Boulder Halt. Somewhere, surely, there were riders, men with long guns and faces of stone, a rope looped over a saddle horn; men carrying with them memories of four men in dusters and yellow slickers, and of a young girl shot in the back in the arms of her father.

'Jesus, no!' Owen Lawson said through his teeth. And common sense told him that it was too soon, that men must be summoned, a posse sworn in. . . .

'Adam, pull over!' Owen Lawson yelled.

His answer was the fierce lash of the rain, the demonic howl of the rising wind.

He drew his six-gun. The shot fired into the air was like the faint snap of a distant muleskinner's whip. But it was heard, for it was gunfire that both of them feared. He watched Adam twist awkwardly in the saddle, head ducked against the rain, and he waved an arm urgently towards a black stand of trees bowing over a huge, rocky bluff.

Then Owen urged his horse out of the rushing water of the trail, driving it out of the deep ruts and across the slickness of the flattened buffalo grass until the roar of the wind was diminished in the lee of the overhanging rock face and hooves rattled on exposed bedrock and, overhead, the whipping branches of the trees hissed and flapped like black demons reaching for the fugitives with clawing, clutching hands.

'We rest awhile,' Owen said, as Adam clattered into the shelter of the huge rock, dumped the gunny-sack into the dry, leaf-carpeted hollow that had the proportions of a small cave, sat bent over the horn with heaving shoulders. 'Nobody coming. Nobody likely to come, not in this.'

He was down out of the saddle, shaking wetness from his slicker, throwing it across his saddle and reaching into his wet shirt for the makings. Angrily he flung away damp papers, dug deep into his saddle-bag and found dry ones there, huddled against the steaming horse and swiftly rolled a cigarette. At the second attempt the match flared. He blew smoke, turned to toss the Bull Durham to Adam, and felt as if he had been kicked in the stomach when he saw the look in his brother's furious, hate-filled eyes.

'You wouldn't listen, would you?' Adam Lawson said, his voice trembling, out of the saddle now, big fists bunched. 'Tom was against it. I was against it. The only one of us willing to go along with you was young Buck, and he don't know no better except that after Ike you're the oldest and he'd follow you for that reason alone.'

'Cut it out—'

'The hell I will. You were wrong. Tom's dead. Your kid brother's facin' a lynch mob. And for what? For a gunny-sack of cash money that's no damn use to Ike because it ain't going to get to him. You've torn the Lawsons apart, Owen. You reckon Ma'll thank you for that?'

'You finished?'

Owen snapped the words, saw his brother jerk, the dark eyes widen. He saw the mouth open to spit more angry words, and he stepped forward, drove the heel of his hand against Adam's chest and slammed him back against the rock face.

'Now you listen to this, feller—'

'No, damn you, Owen, I'm through listening, I—'

'All right, what then?'

His fist tightened on Adam's wet shirt front. He twisted, shook, heard his brother's teeth click, growled again, deeper, feeling something rise within him and knew it was the sickness of cold fury.

'All right,' he said again, 'what then, Adam? You're through listening, so what now? You got some bright ideas? You see a way out of this damn mess? Because if you do, you tell me, right now. But, by God, if you're shooting your mouth off just to hear the sound of your own voice and maybe ease your conscience by letting me know you wanted no part of this, then you'd best keep your damn mouth shut – you hear me?'

Adam took a deep shuddering breath. His right hand came up, clamped on Owen's wrist. Their eyes met, locked.

'I said,' Owen gritted, 'do you hear me?'

'I hear you.'

'And?'

'Why didn't we leave it to Ike's owlhoot pards? We know four of them are hangin' around Austin. They're waiting, biding their time. They get the chance, they'll rig a rope and rip the side off the jail, maybe bust in there with a buckboard—'

'All for nothing.'

'He'd be out. Free. Ain't that what you and Ma want?'

29

'No. We want him out of jail, yes – but out legal, a lawyer speaking for him, a judge deciding he's not guilty. I want him walking out with his head high so he can leave the owlhoot, ride home, start living decent.'

'Then that's too much. You asked, so I'll tell you: there is no way out.'

Angrily, Owen shook off his brother's hand and stepped away. He bent to pick up his tobacco sack, took a deep draw of the cigarette that had remained in his right hand during the explosive words. Then he flicked it away into the rain that was sweeping past the bluff.

'All right,' he said, looking sideways at Adam, keeping a tight rein on his temper. 'If there's no way out then I guess you'll be riding home.'

'What?'

'That's what you want, isn't it?'

'I. . . .'

'You push hard,' Owen went on remorselessly, 'you'll make it in a couple of days, get a good hot supper down you, be able to sit down alongside the stove, tell her what we've been doing.'

'A couple of days,' Adam said, his eyes haunted, 'he'll be dead.'

'Ike? Or Buck?'

Adam swallowed, spat drily.

'You've got maybe ten thousand bucks in that sack,' Owen said. 'What we set out to do, we've done. Almost. So close. So damn close. . . .' He shook his head, deliberately let the tension seep out of his muscles, went on. 'All right, we paid a high price. But why stop, Adam? Wouldn't it be better for four of us to ride home to Ma, instead of just you and me?'

'Four?' Adam said hoarsely. 'Goddammit, Owen, Tom's dead, Buck's in jail and—'

'Maybe I'm not thinking straight, but at least I'm trying to work this out. So let me worry about Buck. You use that money to finish the job.'

Adam Lawson pushed himself away from the rock overhang, ran shaking hands down his rain washed face, his dark beard; looked at his bone-weary horse, then back to the heavy gunny-sack he had tossed into the slick wet leaves under trees.

'Two days' ride to Austin, at most, following the railroad all the way,' Owen said, his voice deliberately quiet. 'Make sure you get there. If you can locate Ike's owlhoot pards, tell them why you're there, tell them to back off. Then use the cash to fix up that lawyer for Ike. When all that's taken care of, you telegraph the good news.'

Adam's head shot around. 'Telegraph? Where the hell to?'

'Boulder Halt.'

'Hell, Owen, you can't go back there.'

'Only one of the four men who robbed that bank

31

in the Halt was clean shaven, and he's in jail. I get rid of this beard, leave that slicker behind—'

'The marshal was in the bank.'

'His back was turned. I bent a six-gun barrel over his skull.'

'Jesus, he came out, looked straight at you.'

'He climbed up off the floor, muzzy-headed, squinted through the rain at a bearded man wearing a slicker and a black hat.' Owen grinned bleakly, and held out his hand. 'Give me your hat, kid.'

'You're crazy.'

'You said it yourself: Buck's in jail. So come up with a better idea – or give me that hat.' Impatiently, he took off his own hat, held it out; waited.

Adam Lawson swore softly. He swept off his grey hat. When he shook his head, dark hair tumbled over his eyes. He swept it back with his fingers, took Owen's hat, put it on.

'All right,' Owen Lawson said. 'That took care of, there ain't no sense you hanging around.'

'Listen,' Adam said, 'maybe you think what I've been sayin' is pretty rough—'

'Forget it. Tom was your twin brother. I didn't expect thanks.'

'Yeah, well, I'm makin' sure you know I'm dead against this, always have been – but when I agreed to ride with you that meant we were all in it, together.'

'We're still in it together – what's left of us.' Owen deliberately met the simmering anger in Adam's eyes, said quietly, 'And I know you'll do your best.'

'As long as I'm able, as long as I've got breath in my body. As long as Ma needs me.'

'She'd appreciate that. I'm telling you now that I do, too. But what you're doing, the risks you're taking, there's no guarantee of success. So I'm asking you now, Adam: if things go wrong . . . if Ike don't make it . . . you know what you've got to do?'

For an instant, Adam hesitated. He said, 'Owen, we've got enough trouble without you goin' back there huntin' for more—'

'I asked a question.'

Again, Adam hesitated. Then he nodded.

'Sure,' he said hoarsely. 'I know what to do.'

Wordlessly, the two brothers clasped hands.

Chapter Four

'I understand your feelings,' Nat Kimball said. 'But there'll be no lynching. That boy'll be tried by Judge Haynes in a couple of weeks' time – and you know damn well that's for bank robbery, not murder.'

'If my daughter lives,' Frank Warren said. 'According to the doc, she'll be lucky to make it through the night. If she dies. . . .'

'If she dies, the boy gets tried for murder,' Kimball said.

The oil lamp flickered as the wind rattled the timbers and a fierce draught hissed under the jailhouse door. It was mid-morning, but low clouds tearing across the stormy skies blocked out the weak sun and turned the day to permanent dusk. Kimball had his booted feet up on the scarred desk. Deputy Jim Folsom was standing with his backside to the glowing stove, his clothes steaming as he teetered on the heels and toes of his muddy boots. Both lawmen were keeping a wary eye on Frank Warren, who had stormed in with murder in his eyes and a sawn-off shotgun gripped in his soft, banker's hands.

'There's townsfolk out there agree with me,' Warren said. He dashed rainwater from his face with a shaking hand, waggled the shotgun. 'Every damn one of them hardworking men has lost money. They want that kid brought out and hanged from the nearest tree. Then they want you two men out there, doing the job you're paid for, and right now that's riding after the two bandits that got away.'

'They seem mighty eager to let me know what they want,' Kimball said, 'without exactly fallin' over themselves to form a posse.'

'Hah!' Frank Warren barked derisively. 'Give and take, Kimball. You show willing, they'll rally round. Send that boy out – and if you need help pulling on the end of that rope, you just let them know.'

'For the last time,' Kimball said with a sudden hard edge to his voice, 'there'll be no hanging, Warren, so if any of your friends've got ideas about bustin' in here after my prisoner—'

'There are no ifs.' A sudden, hard smile twisted the banker's lips. 'Either you bring him out, or they come and take him – and there's no way two

of you can hold this jail against a bunch of determined men.'

Over by the stove, Jim Folsom spat drily. 'I
guess that's why they walked or rode over to Sean
Flanagan's place, damn near bust down his doors
in their hurry to pour themselves some backbone.'

Nat Kimball's spurs scraped across the desk
and his booted feet hit the floor with a thud. He
stood up, watching with amusement as the
banker hastily stepped back a pace.

'Your bank's on the way to Flanagan's saloon,
Warren. You take yourself over there, tell those
men loud and clear what I just told you.'

'It's out of my hands I—'

'After that I suggest you close your premises for
the day and head over to Doc Howard's. Last I
heard, your daughter was doin' fine, but gunshot
wounds can take an ugly turn and before you
know it. . . .'

He left the words hanging, busied himself shuf-
fling papers back and forth on his desk until the
door slammed hard enough to shake the walls and
rattle fire irons. Then, palms flat on the scarred
timber, he looked up to meet the enquiry in his
deputy's level grey eyes.

'Ain't that a mite risky, Nat? Sendin' him over
to the doc's?'

'My pa had a sayin',' Kimball said, 'about a
careless man not seein' the wood for the trees.

That just about sums up Frank Warren.' He
clapped his hat on his head, winked at Folsom,
and headed for the door. 'Keep an eye on the kid.
I'm about to talk some sense into those fellers
over at Flanagan's.'

Owen rode into town with the wind behind him,
whipping the horse's tail along its withers and
turning his back to ice so that repeatedly he
cursed the lack of the yellow slicker.

Then in an instant, the silent curses were
turned to muttered thanks to the Almighty that
he hadn't worn the giveaway yellow coat as he
splashed through the mud to tuck in alongside
the plankwalk for shelter and was almost close
enough for the big horse to step on the town
marshal as he emerged from the saloon.

Eyes met, locked. The marshal swung away,
still looking back at Owen. Then he made a wide,
sweeping gesture, clearly demonstrating his
disgust at the filthy weather – and with a rueful
grin he turned up the collar of his mackinaw and
pounded away down the plankwalk.

Owen felt the hard stiffness in the muscles of
his shoulders and jaw relax. The first big test.
Came sooner than he'd expected. Done with just
as fast, and with the outcome exactly what he
needed. Hell, he was due some kind of luck after
the mess they'd made robbing the bank – but this

was luck of his own making, a calculated risk that had got him back into the town of Boulder Halt and that much closer to springing Buck from jail.

He flicked his eyes across the street to the hotel, caught movement in a ground-floor window and instantly remembered the woman with blonde hair; wondered why thoughts of her had come to him unbidden, what part she would play in what was to come. For there was much to come, he knew, before the Lawsons – or what was left of them – could turn their backs on the dark chapter in their lives that was the town of Boulder Halt, the incident at Frank Warren's bank. . . .

Then he was passing the saloon, half listening to men's voices raised in heated argument, knowing this was to be expected and not feeling too much concern. Down the street, Stolt's Livery beckoned. A block before it, the warm vapour from sizzling slabs of beef topped with fried onion drifted like mist from the door of Annie's Café to be torn ragged by the wind.

Across from the café a door slammed, as the marshal reached the jail and popped into his office like a jack-rabbit down a hole.

Owen's belly rumbled.

He nudged with his knee, sent the horse at an angle across the street and paid for leaving shelter with an icy blast that threatened to take off his ears. He hunched his shoulders without much relief, rode with reluctance past the steamed-up windows of the café, squinted ahead to the livery barn.

And now he was level with the jail.

He glanced across with his head ducked; saw a tall figure pass in front of an oil lamp, a haze of cigarette smoke, the glint of weapons in a rack. No sign of Buck. But that meant nothing. They'd have him out back, caged like an animal in a stinking strap-steel cell.

Unless . . .

Owen swung his head away, deliberately blanking his mind to the sudden, terrible image of a quirt cracking across a horse's flank to send it lunging forward, a young boy swinging from a hang-rope, his body twisting in the fierce wind and rain. He forced his eyes to look ahead, felt the prick of hot tears he told himself were caused by the wind – even though his back was to the storm – and deliberately squeezed his eyes tight shut, took a deep, shaky breath.

When he opened his eyes again it was as if night had fallen: unbidden, his horse had turned towards the sweet smell of hay and fresh oats and come to rest in the dimness of the livery barn's runway.

'I guess he knows what he wants, knows where to get it.'

'Looks like he does, at that,' Owen agreed,

swinging stiffly to the ground. He felt his knees crack, winced, shook himself like a dog and turned to Ed Stolt, the hostler, who was watching him with shrewd blue eyes set in a face like the kernel of an over-ripe nut.

'Bad weather keeps men at home, but with that taken into account this town seems too damn quiet.' Owen flicked a coin to the old man, saw it glint in the air to be caught deftly and disappear into an overall pocket.

'A man rolls out of bed late, ain't no use complainin' if he misses all the excitement.'

'And what's your idea of excitement, old-timer?'

The hostler's eyes were chill and unnervingly keen. 'Four galoots held up Frank Warren's bank, plugged his daughter, made off with a heap of cash.' He cast a glance at Owen's horse, squinted an eye at Owen's sodden clothing and said, 'But you'd've seen 'em for sure, ridin' in from the direction you did.'

'Four men, you say?' Owen said thoughtfully, and frowned and pursed his lips.

'Did I?'

'As I recall.'

'Four robbed the bank, is what I said. What I disremembered to mention was that only two rode out.'

'I think suspicion's got you by the throat, old-timer, told you to bait a trap. So, what happened to the others? Gunned down?'

'One of 'em. Stone cold. Kimball's got the other one locked up – for now.'

'A familiar story of Western justice, so let me guess,' Owen said, 'the kid's in there until the man whose daughter was murdered—'

'Plugged,' Stolt said flatly, and his blue eyes flashed cold fire and his mouth twisted as he waited.

'Yeah, so you said,' Owen said as sudden hope uncoiled to wrap itself warmly around his chilled soul. 'But I guess you disremembered to tell me she's not dead.'

'Not yet,' said the hostler, and turned to spit. 'Lucifer and the Lord're having a set to. Ain't no tellin' which way it'll go.'

'So while they're fighting it out,' Owen said, 'why don't you start earning that silver dollar by looking after my horse, rub down, feed, so forth, and I'll wander up the street and give myself the same treatment?'

'Sure.' Stolt grinned with his mouth, reached for the reins, held them looped in a knotty hand. 'But if I was in your boots I'd first wander over to the saloon, listen to Frank Warren talkin' up a storm. The Lord and Lucifer ain't the only two fightin' it out. Warren and the marshal are powerful men on different sides of the fence, but with the banker's girl close to death you'd be pushed to

41

find an onlooker gives a hoot about what's right or wrong.'

'Maybe I'll do that.' Owen turned away, was already into the icy rain sweeping across the big doors when the old man called after him.

'You talk to anybody on your way in, stranger?'

Owen stopped, turned, stared without speaking.

'I guess that's a no,' Ed Stolt said, 'so it must've been something I said, only—'

'Only you plumb disremember saying it,' Owen said – and waited.

'Hell,' the hostler said, 'ain't that just the truth? For the life of me, I can't recall tellin' you the feller over at the jail Frank Warren aims to hang is just a young kid, but you come straight out with it, so. . . .'

He turned away with a crafty sidelong look, and to the clatter of hooves and the rustle of booted feet through dry straw he led Owen's horse away between the stalls lining the gloomy runway.

Chapter Five

By midday the wind had blown itself out. The sullen clouds slowed their trek westward, then swiftly banked up into a solid grey mass. The rain that had been driven across the prairie in stinging grey curtains became a steady downpour; in an hour, the main street of Boulder Halt was a river of churning muddy water.

In those conditions, Marshal Nat Kimball's posse remained unformed, for the lawman knew damn well that chasing two armed bank robbers across waterlogged grassland where visibility was cut to no more than a hundred yards would have been a waste of manpower, and downright risky. Besides, Jim Folsom told him, tongue in cheek, if they waited a mite longer both men would likely get washed back into town by the flood and save them all a whole lot of unnecessary trouble.

The rain did nothing to cool Frank Warren's

anger. Over at the saloon where he still held clamorous court, the men at the bar and at tables dotted about the sawdust-covered floor were dry on the outside – save for one or two damp patches on those who stood beneath the weeping holes in Sean Flanagan's roof – but inwardly heated to fever pitch by the rotgut liquor served by the Irish saloonist and paid for by the smouldering, restlessly pacing banker.

Warren's trip from the jail to Doc Howard's had taken him unannounced into a stuffy front room where the hot smell of strong medication had drained the colour from his florid cheeks. George Howard had emerged from an inner room, carefully locked the door, then told Warren what he had already surmised from a nervous glance at the young woman lying white and still under the sheets: there was no change; two slugs had been removed; the wounds were inflamed, but not infected. Time would heal – or kill.

Warren had left the doc frowning, stroking his jowls and scratching his white hair, had closed the bank for the day then crossed the street to the saloon with his fine black suit torn by the wind and rain. Now, a couple of hours later, the wind gone and the rain a steady drumming on Flanagan's leaking roof, he figured the flushed, sweating men he had been plying with free liquor were about ready to do his bidding.

From his seat over by the streaming window, Owen Lawson, bathed and fed, Adam's shapeless brown Stetson on the table in front of him, an empty jolt glass in his big fist, saw the subtle change in the banker's demeanour. He put down the glass, pushed the hat to one side, eased back in the chair.

The hubbub was abruptly silenced as Frank Warren drew his pistol and slammed the butt hard, three times, on a table. A glass jumped, sloshing liquor. The man at the table jerked back, startled.

Into the sudden quiet Frank Warren said, 'We've talked this all the way through and back again. We've argued in circles while that murderer's reclining in Kimball's jail eating food you paid for, with money that right now is being toted in a wet gunny-sack somewhere out on the trail. That's gone. There's nothing you can do about it.' He broke off, waited, let the silence build as he turned his head to pin each man in turn with a stare that was ferocious. 'Maybe,' he resumed with deceptive softness, 'you're all so goddamn lily-livered there's nothing you can do about *anything*. Maybe. . . .' He took a breath, narrowed his eyes and the hardness of stone was back in his voice when he said, 'But I don't believe that. And I say what we can do is wipe the smug grin off the face of that kid they left behind. Permanent. For keeps.'

Somewhere outside, shutters rattled. The swing doors creaked open, driven by one last gasp of the dying wind. Rain spattered the sawdust.

'Let's hang the bastard before he drowns,' a red-headed wag at the bar quipped, and laughter rippled.

'Do it quick, before Flanagan's poisonous fire-water kills every damn one of us,' said another, a bleary-eyed man with a mournful face, to more drunken mirth.

Over the renewed uproar, Warren yelled, 'All right, how many of you men can I count on?'

The noise subsided. Feet shuffled. Behind the bar, red-bearded Sean Flanagan's grin was twisted with contempt.

'I'll go along to watch the fun,' he said – and the sawn-off scattergun he had last fired at Owen Lawson was slammed on the rough pine bartop.

'Stolt's got more rope than he needs – I'll head over there, meet you at the jail.'

This was the cowboy Owen Lawson had watched enter Annie's Café. He tramped across the room shrugging into his slicker. Behind him as he went out into the rain the swing doors clattered.

Hesitantly, another four men either nodded, grunted their willingness, or raised a hand. Others turned their backs to lean on the bar. One slammed down his glass, averted his eyes from the banker's withering gaze and followed the cowboy.

Warren's eyes swept the room, settled on Owen.

'What about you, stranger?'

'From what I hear, they locked up the kid when all he did was mind some horses.'

'He's an accessory,' Warren said bluntly. 'Guilty by association.'

'I'd say that was up to a judge to decide.'

'Any judge worth his salt would reach that conclusion – so why wait?'

'Because murderers hang, bank robbers get sent to the State Pen. They stay alive.' Owen let that sink in, watched the banker's eyes narrow and said casually, 'How is your daughter, Warren?'

'You have the talk of an educated man, the words of a conservative fool.' Warren came away from the table, walked a pace towards Owen, stopped with legs braced and chin jutting pugnaciously. 'And your face is familiar. I think I've seen you somewhere, my friend.'

'Your thoughts are your affair,' Owen said, 'but like your intentions, they're wrong.'

'No, I rarely make mistakes. . . .' The banker's head was tilted to one side. There was a puzzled look in his eyes. Then, as if realizing that wasting time with Owen would loosen his fragile hold on the men he had softened with drink then lashed with his tongue, he swung around and barked,

'Slim will have that rope by now, so why the hell are you standing there with your mouths open? You think this is a goddamn picnic? You think this is no time to be breaking up a whale of a shindig? Well, let me tell you this: you'll get no more free liquor until this is done – then there'll be plenty for all, as much as you can pour down your throats. So, if you're with me, then let's get down to the jail.'

Without waiting for a reaction, he turned on his heel and walked out of the saloon. Behind him, shifty glances were exchanged. Then, lips clamped into tight, thin lines, nervous hands checking holsters, the four men followed. Sean Flanagan came around the bar untying his apron, flung it carelessly on to a table. Then he swept up his scattergun, winked at Owen and went out into the incessant rain.

Owen tilted his chair, frowned, chewed his lip.

One more lynch-mob to add to his store of bitter, violent memories. A cowboy with a rope, four faltering, jumpy men, a saloonist with a shot-gun and Frank Warren at their head. By the time they got to the jail, they'd be soaked through. In the jail, the glowing stove, a rack of gleaming guns, the marshal and his deputy relaxed but ready, watching the door. Out back. . . .

Out back, Owen knew, there was a frightened kid, lying on an iron bunk, staring out of a strap-steel cage, listening, wide-eyed, to every noise. What he'd hear next would bring him tumbling from that bunk, a frightened animal sensing the approach of the hunter. He'd jump with shock as the door crashed open, stumble backwards to cower against the wall at the alarming stamp of booted feet. And with ears pricked he would hear clearly the words Frank Warren would use to incite his followers and browbeat the two lawmen. Words like 'rope', and 'hang', and 'pay with his life', and 'the law of the West, the only law worth a damn'.

In the heated office, with harsh words pounding one on top of the other and men crowded up against walls and desk and each other, the steam already rising from their soaked clothing, and the tight, electric tension that always comes before the crackling approach of a violent storm – in that atmosphere, it needed one wrong movement to bring the crack of the first shot.

Six men against two, with six-guns blazing in a confined space, their brittle cracks drowned by the thunderous roar of a shotgun.

With a sigh, Owen Lawson came out of his chair, planted the damp Stetson on his head and made for the swing doors. He emerged into an afternoon of gloom to breathe air that was saturated, stood for a moment alert and watchful listening to the beat of the rain on a plankwalk that was black and slippery.

He had known the return to Boulder Halt would be bad. A beard removed and a hat exchanged doesn't change a man's eyes, the way he moves. So far he knew for sure that Ed Stolt over at the livery had seen through the guise and, given time, Frank Warren would remember him as one of the men he had swung to face when he snatched the pistol from the safe and heard the meaty thwack of lead slugs hitting his daughter's body.

But the way things were working out, that knowledge would do him no good because it would come too late. One way or another, Owen would take Buck away from Boulder Halt. He would do it by taking him from the jail if the lynch-mob was beaten back by the two Boulder Halt lawmen. He would do it by taking him from the mob if they came tumbling out of the jail with the boy white-faced and pinioned and the hang-rope swinging.

One way or another.

And he was turning towards the jail, grim faced, when he heard the crack of the first shot.

Chapter Six

Thoughts travel faster than actions, yet some actions are begun without conscious thought. A man's mind can be as fickle as a changeable wind, and there is often no good reason why one sound course is abandoned for another.

Owen Lawson's mind was in a whirl. He had walked out of Sean Flanagan's saloon with the intention of watching events unfold, Yet within seconds he was pounding down the wet plankwalk without fully knowing why. All that registered was the thin snap of the shot followed by the winter sounds of incessant rain and now, as he ran, the roar of his own voice hollering at the man who poked his head out of the mercantile's door, at another who emerged from the tonsorial parlour with his face all lathered with soap, and at the woman who came out of Annie's Café wiping her hands on a cloth and stared wide-eyed towards the jail.

For if the turmoil in his mind allowed room for one urgent thought of crystal clarity, it was that if he was to have any hope of snatching Buck and getting him out of Boulder Halt, he already had his hands full with Kimball, Folsom and the vengeful Frank Warren.

'Get back!' Owen yelled, and was aware of faces turning in his direction, of mouths moving soundlessly as the pounding of his boots drowned words.

'What the hell!' a man blurted – then reeled away with another curse as Owen's shoulder knocked him spinning. The mercantile's door slammed. Annie stayed put, still anxiously wiping her hands, but now there were greasy, unshaven faces in the doorway behind her as men left good hot food to watch the action.

Closer now, a second shot blasted. This one smashed the jail's window, sent glass tinkling on to the plankwalk and, as hot lead hissed through the falling rain and thumped into the wall of Stolt's livery, the watchers suddenly lost interest and scrambled for cover.

He caught a brief glimpse of the blonde woman who had brushed against him as he entered the bank, saw the startling blue of her eyes as she glanced disdainfully in his direction then walked serenely and without haste along the opposite plankwalk in the direction of the hotel.

Then Owen had reached the jail. His boots crunched on broken glass. He could smell acrid gunsmoke. Loud voices smote his ears. He drew his six-gun, took a step back. Mentally apologizing to Buck for what he was about to do, the shock it would cause, his right foot shot out, the leg driving it like a steel piston. Hinges were torn from the frame with a screech of splintering timber. The sole of his boot slammed into the door and it fell inwards. Using it as a ramp, Owen leaped inside.

'Stand still!' he roared. 'Every damn one of you drop those guns!'

There was a shocked silence. Still standing on the wrecked door, Owen was aware of one man groaning. He was flat on his back, his leg pinned under Owen's weight. The three men who had left Flanagan's with great reluctance now fell over themselves as they tried to get out of the way while looking wildly in two directions at the same time. Flanagan grinned crookedly, lowered the shotgun's muzzle. For the second time that morning, Frank Warren was left standing with a cocked pistol in his hand and his face twisted with fury.

'Back off, Frank, it's over.'

This was Marshal Nat Kimball, softly, but in a voice rimmed with steel. As the door crashed inwards and heads turned he had spun out of his chair and grabbed a rifle from the rack. Now he was standing on braced legs and emphasizing the order with a rapid working of the Winchester's lever.

At the same time, Jim Folsom had somehow wormed his way unnoticed around the far side of the desk and was now behind the flustered men.

Folsom coughed, and cocked his pistol.

Owen Lawson eased back the hammer of his .45.

And it was as if the potent liquor that had poured fire into the men tagging along after Frank Warren turned to icy rainwater and trickled out through their boots.

One by one they pouched their weapons and traipsed out through the doorway, the one who had heaved and kicked his way out from under the splintered door limping badly. Sean Flanagan was grinning unconcernedly and whistling through stained teeth as he followed the disgruntled members of the lynch-mob. Looking ahead, Owen figured, to the time they would take grumbling and drowning their sorrows with liquor they would pay for out of their own pockets.

That left Warren.

'Is that the end of it, Frank?'

The banker glared at Kimball, let the question hang then swung on Owen Lawson.

'I knew I'd seen you before,' he growled, and

Owen's blood ran cold. 'I never forget a face. You were in Nogales, three years ago. Bleeding, tied to a wagon, the Rurales playing some Mex card game by lantern light and figuring out what to do with your owlhoot brother.' He paused, snapped his fingers once, twice, frowning. Then his face cleared, and he nodded. 'Ike Lawson, that was his name. And if my memory serves me – as it always does – that man is now in Austin awaiting the fate he escaped in Nogales.'

'Delicately put, for a man burning with bloodlust,' Owen said, conscious of the skin tight over his cheekbones, the relief weakening his knees. 'You managed that without once mentioning a hanging.'

'Whatever this feller's done in the past,' Kimball told Warren, 'when he bust in here he tipped the balance in favour of the law.'

'But ruined a damn fine door,' Jim Folsom said, looking wryly at the wreckage and the opening through which the cold rain now steadily beat.

'His being on the side of the law puts him and me on opposite sides of the street,' Warren said. 'Those whiskey-swilling curs walked out on me, backed off when the going got a mite tough. But do you believe I'll follow suit, Kimball? All right, seems like you've got yourself another man alongside you and Folsom. But do you honestly believe that makes a scrap of difference? Forces me to back off?'

'It's in your best interests. Yours, and your daughter's. She'll get over her wounds, but it won't help her fight back to health if her father's locked away awaiting trial for murder – because you can be damn certain that's the charge I'll make stick if you press ahead with this craziness.'

Warren's eyes were pools of hatred. He swung about, elbowed roughly past Owen and went out into the rain. The marshal watched him impassively, nodded to Jim Folsom who put away his pistol and moved to the shattered door. Owen stepped forward to give the deputy a hand, and together they lifted the heavy timber, leaned it against the wall so that it was covering most of the opening.

'I'll go see Ed Stolt,' Folsom said, brushing his hands and settling his hat. 'When he ain't tendin' horses or cleanin' that old shotgun he's always got his toolbox out fixin' some damn thing or another.'

With the big deputy gone, the room was cold and empty, the damp draught beating back the waves of heat rising thickly from the stove. Kimball came around the desk to kick the door so that it blocked the opening, dug the makings out of his shirt, tossed them to Owen then returned to shift his chair swivel closer to the hissing fire.

Owen sat, fashioned a cigarette, fired a match, slid the tobacco pouch across the desk; watched through a haze of fresh smoke as the marshal rolled his quirly.

And he noted with a faint stir of excitement that Kimball had taken the time to stow the Winchester in the rack. He was sitting forward, mane of black hair brushing the ugly wound behind his ear, elbows on the desk, fingers busy with paper and tobacco. His body was relaxing after a heated situation that had been cooled by the man sitting in front of him. The immediate danger to his prisoner had passed. If he expected more trouble, he would be looking to Frank Warren – but Warren had walked away, and the only route back for the banker was along an empty street slick with mud and naked of cover.

That left the deputy. How long to walk to the livery stable and back? And what would he learn from Ed Stolt?

Nat Kimball was off guard, Owen figured – and with his deputy gone he was alone, though the minutes were ticking away fast. Owen trickled smoke, allowed himself a secretive smile that was a mask covering nerves jumping like Chinese firecrackers. The cigarette glowed in his left hand. He forced his right hand to rest casually on his knee. He was acutely aware of the room heating up and of Kimball's growing torpor, of his own pistol, the precise angle of the butt, the sequence of lightning fast movements needed to draw, cock—

'You look amused,' Kimball said.

A match scraped on the stove's hot metal, flared, and was applied to the fresh tobacco. The marshal blew smoke, waiting.

And suddenly Owen realized that the hooded eyes and lethargic manner hid a mind as sharp as a stropped razor.

'A man rides in looking for work, winds up kicking the jail's door down. Instead of getting slammed in a cell, he's made to feel right at home.' He grinned. 'I guess I always did see the funny side of a situation.'

'How did you find Warren's story?'

'Interesting.'

'For the most part true?'

'Oh, he was right,' Owen said.

'But you changed your ways?'

'I figured I was worth more on the home spread with my widowed ma than over the border pushing up that coarse wire they call grass.'

'The home spread being?'

'North a ways.'

Kimball's mouth tightened.

'So how come you're on hand to stop a lynching, then tell me a story that sounds like a man tryin' hard to make two and two into five?'

Owen cocked an eyebrow. 'Did I do that?'

'What you said was you're worth something to your ma on the home spread. So if a man's appreciated where he's at, his ridin' south looking for work don't exactly add up.'

'We ranch in foothills where rock pokes through the top soil and the cows wear their front teeth down pulling up dry grass,' Owen said. 'In those conditions the fight to scratch a living can turn a good man into a beggar.'

'None that I know would leave their ma to fight on alone,' Kimball said – and waited.

Owen left the comment unanswered, flicked ash, said casually, 'That kid in there tell you his name?'

Kimball leaned back, eased away from stove and desk and suddenly had too much space and, as voices drifted from across the street, Owen saw his advantage slipping away.

'What he told me,' Kimball said, 'was he had four brothers. Three of 'em are workin' a spread up north a ways, the fourth is down Austin way, though the kid didn't say why.'

'Maybe,' Owen said, 'he disremembered,' and was rewarded by a sharp glance from the marshal.

'He didn't say why,' Kimball repeated, then paused, turned to flick his cigarette at the stove and while doing so went on softly, 'but when two men wind up in my office and, without seein' each other, spout tales of a brother down in Austin and a spread "up north a ways", then I get kinda. . . .'

He was still talking when the hand that had

flicked the glowing cigarette at the cooling stove dipped to his holster and in the natural movement of swinging back to the desk he brought up his pistol in a smooth draw that with its speed took away Owen's breath.

'If I was to tell you I recognized you from that fracas outside the bank,' Kimball said, grinning, 'that'd be a lie. But Ed Stolt's already been over here while you were wallowin' in your bath, and what he suggested to me has been confirmed by your actions in here: whatever else you are or have been, Mr Lawson, at robbin' banks you're about the funniest thing I've seen outside of them newfangled vaudeville shows.'

Chapter Seven

As the cell door clanged behind him and the key turned in the lock, Owen said, 'You defended me to Frank Warren, yet all the time you had me figured, knew damn well why I bust down your door.'

Kimball grunted, tossed the keys to the silent Jim Folsom who had returned from the livery with Ed Stolt in tow. 'I take care of one thing at a time. With Warren doin' his damnedest to string up one prisoner, there was no sense me tellin' him I was about to take another.'

Over his shoulder, his eyes torn between the tense figure of Buck and the implacable town marshal, Owen said, 'And what about Tom, my other brother?'

Kimball's eyes were shrouded, unreadable. 'What do you want me to say? You were there, you watched me plug him, saw him go down.'

61

Owen swung around, slammed his raised forearms against the bars so that the tight metal sang, hooked his fingers over one of the cell's steel straps. 'Jesus,' he said, unwilling for the fury and the purpose within him to be swamped by the frustration of a steel cage, 'you're a cold-blooded bastard.'

Folsom uttered a short exclamation of astonishment. Kimball pushed a sack of Bull Durham through the bars, his face suddenly bleak.

'I had my back turned when you walked into the bank with your brothers. Next thing I know I'm down on my knees spittin' blood, Janie Warren's taken a couple of slugs – and now you tell me I'm a cold-blooded bastard!' He laughed without mirth, the tone as hard and as cold as the steel that imprisoned Owen. 'Well, Lawson, it might be worth rememberin' this cold-blooded bastard's what stands between you and a hang rope. If you plan on bustin' out of here and put me out of action in the proceedings, you'll come up against your hot-blooded friend Warren and his pals.' He turned away, shaking his head. 'I'll put a month's salary on it: you and your kid brother won't reach the town limits.'

The office door slamming shut behind the town marshal and his deputy punctuated the ugly words.

Owen Lawson turned away, faced his brother.

'My God, what the hell kind of mess. . . !'

He choked on the words, shook his head helplessly, took two long strides and swiftly embraced
the youngster. Then he stepped back, held the
boy's shoulders, looked into his blue eyes.

'I should have listened, out there in the woods.
You were all against it.'

'Not me!'

'Hell, you've got the wildness of any young kid,
you couldn't know—'

'Where's Adam?'

'Heading south. With luck, he'll get there in
time.'

'In this rain, the plains in flood?'

The sharp, bitter exchange of words was broken
off as both men listened to the steady drum of
rain on the tin roof, the knocking from the outer
office where Ed Stolt was working on the door.

'The weather that delays Adam,' Owen said
carefully, 'will also delay the circuit judge.'

'No!' Buck twisted away from Owen's hands,
turned away to pace across the cell, back again.
'It's no good, Owen. Before we rode out I heard you
talkin' to Ma. The trial's over. Ike's guilty. All
they're awaitin' on is the date for the hangin', the
man with the rope.'

Warily, Owen said, 'What else did you hear?'

'Huh?'

'There was a mite more said, mostly by Ma, and

her voice is sharp enough to cut through rimrock.'
He shrugged, experiencing a lightening sense of
relief as Buck's eyes registered puzzlement. 'It's
not important, kid. I guess what you'd already
overheard was more than enough to paint a
pretty grim picture.'

'Grim?' Buck said. His voice held the thin edge
of despair. He swung away again, took a couple of
aimless paces, turned around and with his hands
spread and his eyes desperate said, 'Owen, with
this weather it'll be dark in a couple of hours. I
know eavesdroppin's a bad habit, but I couldn't
help overhearin' that banker. He'll be back – and
if we don't get out of here there'll be a Lawson
hanged in Austin, two more strung up here in the
Halt—'

'Quit that!'

The harsh command shocked the boy into
silence. His hands fell. He took a breath, shook his
head.

'All right,' he said with a twisted smile. 'Back
there in the woods you told us the family was your
responsibility. Well, with one dead and two in jail
I reckon you've done pretty good so far, so I'll leave
it to you.'

Owen grunted, feeling the cruel impact of
distasteful truth like the sharp pain of a knifing.
He fumbled in his pocket, dug out the marshal's
tobacco sack, fashioned a cigarette. When it was

fired up he let the first smoke out through parted lips in a gust of expelled breath. Then he looked at Buck, sitting disconsolately on the edge of the bunk, and smiled crookedly.

'I guess what Ma said after you closed up your ears was important – and now's a good time for some plain talking.'

Tom Lawson's lean frame was bent like a green sapling in a storm, his face lined with strain. He had swung his legs off the bed, located his stiff wet boots, pulled them on with an effort that left him drenched in cold sweat. Now he was buckling on his gunbelt, his lower lip tight between his teeth as the hot sweet agony in his ribs set his senses swimming.

He was standing, but swaying drunkenly, when the outer door clicked open and the stout figure of Doctor George Howard walked in.

The doc grunted. 'I've seen new-born calves stand straighter.'

'Yeah, I had you figured for one of them sawbones they call when an animal goes down with the fever,' Tom said through his teeth.

'If Kimball's slug hadn't hit your six-shooter, slammed it against your ribs, I'd be wearing my black coat and driving the hearse.'

'A man of many parts.' Tom forced a grin, then winced.

'I do my best for a small town.' Howard's blue eyes, behind wire-framed spectacles, were watching him critically. 'One way is by keeping my lip buttoned. The marshal knows you're alive, but he told me to keep it under my hat and that's what I've done.' He pursed his lips. 'You know they took the youngster. Have you been lying there planning a jail break?'

'Yeah, thought I'd bust in there, sock the marshal on the jaw, disarm his deputy, walk out with the kid.'

'Hmph. Your brother's tried that.'

'And?'

'And now there's two of them sharing a cell.'

Tom winced, remembering the hail of bullets outside the bank, Owen and Adam hammering towards the edge of town as he lay in agony in the wet mud. 'He got a name, this other brother?'

Howard shrugged. 'If he has, no one's telling. All I can tell you is that he's some years older than you, and clean shaven.'

'No. Buck's the only one of us without a beard.'

'Then subterfuge was planned.'

'If you mean trickery, I guess you're right. But it looks like it didn't work.'

'No, and I believe you were jesting about the jail break,' Howard said. 'If, on the other hand, you were speaking the truth, then I have a duty to prevent you leaving this house.'

'Doc, the only thing I've been planning is how to get home without falling off my horse. Things turned out bad enough without making them a heap worse. Owen can take care of himself, and Buck. Me, I—' He broke off, flicked a swift glance at the door as a soft sound reached his ears, turned to Howard with his eyes wide, questioning.

'Yes. She's alive. Two bullets went in below the right shoulder, missed the lung, broke a rib on the way out.'

'Thank the Lord!'

'Indeed. Frank Warren is about to marry the delightful Laura Beckett. He would dearly love his daughter to be at the wedding.'

'Pluggin' her was a mistake,' Tom said. 'She—'

'Young man, don't bore me. Janie's on the mend. All I want now is your word that you intend leaving town.'

'Hell, what choice do I have?'

'Hmph. Not a direct answer to the question.' He shrugged. 'Well, your horses were taken to Ed Stolt's livery.'

'Is he a compassionate man?'

Howard smiled with his mouth. 'He won't stand in your way.'

'Then I'll be off.'

'Your duster's on a peg in the other room.'

'I won't be needing it.'

Unsteady steps took him to the door. Aware of

Howard following close behind he eased it open, crossed the outer room, smelling antiseptic and a faint perfume; hearing the soft sounds of a woman breathing.

'She's still weak. Go, shut the door quickly.'

Tom nodded; eased open the door; stepped out into a chilling downpour. Breathing tightly, pain lancing through his ribs, he pulled the door shut and leaned against it. He tilted his head back so that the cold rain washed over his face. His heart was pounding.

The evening came early bringing with it the blackness of night, the darkness hastened and intensified by the lowering clouds and the incessant rain that had beaten down on Boulder Halt throughout the long winter's day. Lights made hazy by the downpour shone their haloed warmth from the misted windows of the saloon, the livery barn and Annie's Café, their reflections streaks of brightness on the glistening yellow mud and streams of water that poured down the main street.

At the rear of the jail, lamplight glowed in the passage where the floor was beaded with damp. The light washed across the cell's dirt floor in thin stripes painted by the bars and melted into the gloom without reaching the bunk where Owen lay smoking, the other where Buck lay shivering under a thin blanket with his hands behind his head, his face intent.

In the half-hour since he had admitted the need for plain talking Owen had backed off and talked instead about this and that of little consequence, mostly trying to set his brother's mind at ease by imparting the philosophy that a man's life was never plain sailing, was always built on platforms of the unexpected.

'Which means,' he had finished, 'that no matter how you have all this figured, something you haven't anticipated can come walking in through that door and either kick you in the teeth or pat you on the back and hand you a big fat cigar.'

That had brought the flicker of a smile to Buck's face, and with the feeling that his aimless talk about nothing in particular had calmed frayed nerves and at least put the boy in a position to think, Owen finally got to the point.

He paused, let the silence build until he knew Buck was pricking his ears in the gloom, then said, 'Getting back to what you told me about overhearing Ma talking—'

'Forget it.'

'No. You listen, and listen hard—'

'But I was wrong. Being responsible for the family doesn't mean you get it right every time. Your aim was to get Ike out of jail, you went after the money the only way you could and you did it for Ma—'

'No. I did it for me, and I did it for Ike.'

Light from the lantern glinting in Buck's eyes winked out as he narrowed them, and frowned.

'But ... sure, you told us that. We knew we were doin' it for Ike. But then you said Ma was looking to you to bring him home and—'

'That's right. But I was lying. The bit you missed hearing back home was Ma tearing strips off my hide for even contemplating going after that wicked bastard.'

'Wicked?'

'Both of us. Him, and me. But a couple of years back, down in Nogales when the Rurales were crawling all over us, he saved my life. That lesson made me see sense, put me on my horse and pointed me towards home. And your ma's heart softened. Maybe she saw the change in me was permanent. Maybe she'd always figured I was hanging on big, bad Ike's coat-tails out of hero worship, bravado, one day I'd see how crazy that kind of behaviour is in a grown man. Maybe ... Anyhow, when I got home, and all the time I was working the ranch, I was in debt to your brother. That's why we rode south, you and me, Adam, Tom ... And that's why Tom's dead, why you and me are freezing to death in a cell, why. . . .'

He looked across the cell. Buck's eyes were closed. The exhausted kid was asleep.

'I should have left the whole damn shebang to

Ike's owlhoot pards,' he said softly. 'They could handle it better than me – for all I know he's already sprung, and Adam's on a wasted journey. But no, I was a fool, and all it's got me is a heap of trouble—'

The passage door clicked open.

Warm light from the office outlined the tall figure of Nat Kimball and a slip of yellow paper.

He said, 'I hate doing this, Lawson, but I've brung you more bad news.'

Chapter Eight

'What Warren's decided on – with Flanagan's help,' the cowboy said, around a mouthful of tough, fried beef, 'is the hour after midnight when Kimball's tired and on his own, Folsom maybe out takin' a break, packin' in some vittles.'

'Yeah, but what I want to know,' said the gaunt man with the mournful face, his gaze fuddled, 'is if we do drag them two bank robbers out, do we hang 'em, or drown 'em?'

The red-headed wag grinned wickedly and pointed vaguely upwards with his greasy knife. 'That's a damn fool question. We string 'em up in this rain they'll likely drown before they choke anyways – but either way they're dead.'

Annie came out of the kitchen, a cloth over her arm, face flushed and damp under straggly hair.

'And what I want to know is why you three don't shut your fool mouths and start usin' your brains? You know all Frank Warren'll get you is trouble, and for what?'

'Jesus Christ, Annie,' the cowboy said, his eyes hot. 'The man's gettin' set to marry Laura Beckett, and his daughter's been shot daid. Now if that was me—'

'She's alive,' Tom Lawson said from his seat by the window.

'Hell,' the wag said, 'I heard somebody call for Jesus, but I didn't realize he was settin' right there amongst us all the time.'

Annie wandered over, gave the table in front of Tom a quick wipe with the filthy cloth, flicked back a dark strand of damp hair and said, 'What makes you so sure?'

Tom grinned ruefully. With his voice raised for the benefit of the other listeners he said, 'If you had my ribs, you'd know. My horse threw me on the way into town. I called in at the doc's, got myself strapped up, saw the girl on the way out.'

'Talk to her?'

This was the wag, and Tom shook his head. 'She's still unconscious, but she had colour, looked like she was breathing fine.'

'All right,' the cowboy said, 'so Warren neglected to tell us his gal's alive, but I don't see as it makes all that much difference. Since them fellers robbed the bank we're all out of pocket, some of us damn near bust.'

There were murmurs of agreement, some puzzled looks tossed in Tom's direction, then they turned back to their food and a rambling discussion on the merits and demerits and the whys and wherefores of what they were about to do – most of the talk heated, most of it leading in one direction and ending with two bodies twisting and swinging in the driving rain.

And they would do it, Tom knew, because ... well, he thought, pushing back his empty plate and reaching for the makings, because that's the way it was always done. A man stole a horse and got caught, his neck was stretched. It was anyone's guess where bank robbery and wounding fitted into the scale of misdemeanours, but it was surely as bad as taking a man's horse, very likely worse because more people were affected.

As Annie drifted away to spread the filth from her damp cloth on to the empty tables as she diligently wiped while casting suspicious glances at the stranger, he squinted, narrow-eyed, at the three men through the smoke of his cigarette and the steam billowing from the kitchen, calculated that if the lynch mob got together and made its move in the hours after midnight then he was pushed for time.

He had to get in and out fast, get Owen and Buck out of town before it was too late.

But with cracked ribs and prowess with a six-gun that, he suspicioned, was unlikely to match that of Marshal Nat Kimball and his capable deputy, he was no more looking forward to walking into the jail than he had been to robbing Warren's bank.

In a somewhat thoughtful and not too optimistic frame of mind he mashed out his cigarette and left the café, pausing for a few moments on the sidewalk to look about him, the dull murmur of voices from Flanagan's saloon a grim reminder that the three men in Annie's would have plenty of drunken support.

The main street of Boulder Halt was a quagmire of glistening yellow mud flattened by the rain. To his right, the front of the mercantile was in darkness, blinds drawn. Rainwater was running in steady streams down the street's false fronts to form a river hissing across the plankwalk. Beyond the mercantile, a dim light glowed from the street window of Ed Stolt's office, set inside the livery stable and alongside its open doors.

And across the street from the mercantile, spaced midway between Annie's place and Stolt's stables, the jail. Well lit. The door, Tom noted with interest, off its hinges and only half covering the opening. Owen's doing, he figured, but as the sound of hammering reached his ears he knew it was already being repaired, and would shortly be locked.

Absently he took out the makings, realized what he was doing, stowed them away again with a muttered oath. His heart was thumping beneath strapped ribs. His breathing was tight, partly from necessity, mostly from apprehension. He made an effort, forced his mind to concentrate on what needed doing, not on the calamity he would be responsible for if things went wrong. Tried to look ahead, one step at a time, until he could clearly see the three of them riding abreast across the flooded prairie with Boulder Halt no more than a bleak memory.

Riding. That meant horses. So, the first step was to make sure that when they came busting out of the jail, their mounts were waiting.

Tom Owen set his jaw, and turned towards Ed Stolt's livery barn.

'Where'd he send this from?'

Owen was up against the cold strap steel, talking quietly while the kid slept, the damp yellow paper limp in his hand.

'Whistle stop down the line. Another one horse town.'

'Far?'

'Twenty, thirty miles.'

'That close.' It was a comment, not a question. Owen was thinking of the desperate ride into the teeth of the storm. The cold, then the dying wind.

A horse, head-hung and wrung-out, hooves slipping and sliding as Adam forced it to follow the gleaming rails into the gathering gloom as nightfall and the incessant downpour merged into blackness.

'Lucky there was a telegraph.' Nat Kimball shrugged. 'Or maybe not. News like that ain't never welcome.' His eyes remained fixed on Owen as he said, 'I guess there's no point in keepin' things from you. There were two wires, Lawson. The one addressed to me kinda piles on the misery.'

'Yeah?'

'The judge who tried your brother is in a hurry, and set on using the railroad like he always does. His train pulls into the halt at three tomorrow afternoon.'

Owen's laugh was bitter. 'Fifteen hours to a necktie party,' he said, and shook his head as he flipped open the yellow paper.

'IKE DEAD'.

'Always was one for plain speaking, Adam,' Owen said, his face giving nothing away as he read for the fourth or fifth time the two stark words on the telegraph slip.

'It explains some things I was puzzling over,' Kimball said. 'The way you went about the job I

77

never did see you fellers as bank robbers. So I couldn't figure out why. But if your brother was heading down the line with that stolen cash, then it all begins to make sense. Ike Lawson awaitin' the hang rope in Austin; a good lawyer costing a heap of money. . . .' He waited, absently scratching his jaw.

'Yeah,' Owen said with bitterness in his voice. 'And it all turned out to be a waste of time.'

'Time?' Kimball's laugh was ironic. 'Your brother was plugged in the act of robbin' a bank. You and your kid brother're in jail. I just told you the judge comin' up from Austin is the one hanged Ike Lawson, and when he gets here he'll be faced with two more Lawsons. Hell, he won't bother shuckin' his coat before passin' sentence – and all you can say is what you done was a waste of time!'

'Keep your voice down,' Owen said.

'Jesus!' Kimball swung away, face tight.

'No, you don't understand,' Owen blurted. 'The kid's sick.'

'Sick?'

'He was coming down with fever before we left home, but he didn't want to be left behind so he convinced me he'd be OK. But hanging around in the woods, in this weather. . . .' All the time he was speaking Owen was watching Kimball, swiftly weighing up his chances if he acted now, knowing that Adam had sent the wire blind but

78

wondering why there was nothing, no message, just those two words.

So, with nothing else to go on, and Warren sure to make another move, it had to be soon. If he could get Kimball to open the cell – but not yet, not until he'd talked to Buck, not until they'd worked out some way of getting the jump on the two lawmen.

'He went to sleep,' he said, striving to put into his voice carefully masked concern, 'and when I shook him, tried to wake him—'

'Are you saying the kid's real bad?'

'I'm saying I don't know – but I do know he needs a doc.'

Kimball chewed his lip, his eyes glittering in the gloom as they darted from Owen to Buck. Then he grunted, turned to the door and flung over his shoulder, 'I'll get Doc Howard to have a look at him, but when he comes in there'll be two of us watching you like hawks so—'

The door slammed, cutting off the rest.

Buck jerked upright on the bunk, peered about blearily, said, 'Wha . . . what?'

'Lie down.'

'What the hell was that?'

'You're sick. Kimball's gone for the doc.'

'Nah, I'm tired, that's all.'

'But he doesn't know that. If you want out of here, lie down, breathe like you're a dying man.'

'I ain't never listened to a dying man.'

Owen smiled grimly. 'Let's hope I'm not the first.'

Buck came off the bunk in a cat-like roll. 'What in Hades are you plannin', Owen?'

Owen used his palm to push him lightly in the chest, eased him back to a sitting position on the edge of the cornhusk mattress, looked at the flaring panic in the boy's eyes.

'You tell me, kid,' he said, shaking his head in feigned helplessness. 'One way or another we've got to get the hell out of here before Warren and his cronies mount up and ride their broncs straight over the marshal and his deputy. But me, I must be getting old. I'm plumb out of ideas.'

'You!'

'That's right.'

'But – but it was you figured out how to help Ike, made all them plans, whipped all of us into shape.'

'Turns out I didn't do too well.' He touched the yellow telegraph slip poking out of his shirt pocket. 'This came from Adam. You never did know Ike well, so maybe it won't bother you too much, but Adam turned back before he got near Austin, because the hangman had already done his work.'

Buck bit his lip.

'Poor Ma. . . .'

'Yeah. She comes first, always has done – and right now we're wasting time on useless talk.'

'Right.' Buck nodded, ran his fingers through his hair, looked fast around the cell. 'Ain't nothing we can use for weapons, and we'll be up against two tough *hombres* with six-guns.' He bounced on the bunk, felt under the mattress, ran his hands along the metal frame and looked questioningly at Owen.

'No. Take too long to break up.' Owen frowned, sucked his teeth.

'Maybe we could split, so when they come in we jump them from two sides.'

'Sounds good, but there'll be three of them—' Owen broke off as if pondering, watching Buck out of the corner of his eye while keeping one ear open for the returning marshal.

'Yeah, that's right,' Buck breathed. 'The doc'll come in, walk over, take a look at me and—'

Owen nodded. 'Yeah, that's right – so there is one way.'

Buck grinned, waiting. 'Plumb out of ideas, huh?'

'Good ones, anyhow. But you gave it to me when you mentioned the doc, the way he's sure to act when he walks in.' He narrowed his eyes. 'Problem is, this one'll be tough going and you'll be doing most of the hard work, taking all the risks – so if you're not sure. . . .'

A lie to boost the kid's confidence, Owen thought ruefully. The risk would be his, not Buck's because, of the two of them, he would be totally exposed. And the risk was big, too big, he knew that; knew it, hated the thought of what could happen, what more than likely would happen when they came up against Kimball and Folsom. But with Warren a growing threat, the judge just fifteen hours away, their situation was desperate. Hell, they had no choice, and better, surely, to die fighting than choking in agony at the end of a rope.

The boy was grinning, pushing out his chest. 'Spell it out, Owen, then leave it to me.'

'You're a good kid. I'm counting on you – and so's Ma.'

With a movement as swift as any fast draw, Owen reached into his right boot and came up holding his cut down Bowie knife with a blade made slender by years of honing.

'When they open the cell and let the doc in, Kimball and Folsom will stand back with their six-guns drawn. If you do like I said – lie back, breathe like a dying man – the doc's forced to bend close, open your shirt.'

'And suddenly he's got a knife at his throat and the lawmen back off and we up and walk straight out the door,' Buck said eagerly.

'Easy now,' Owen cautioned. 'I've not set eyes on

the doc, could be he's a big feller, tough as rawhide. But no matter what, big or small, you'll need to keep the blade in close, keep the doc between you and them.'

'Sure, and with you on the other side of the cell—'

'They'll be caught looking two ways.'

'And it'll be all over in minutes,' Buck said. 'With the doc as a shield we make it to the livery—'

'They take the horses there?'

'Yep, I heard them talkin'.'

'So – are you all set?'

'Sure – and this is going to work,' Buck said.

'It'd better work,' Owen said, and tossed him the knife. 'Get down on that bunk, kid – here they come.'

Chapter Nine

With a full belly, Tom Lawson mused wistfully, the most natural thing would be for him to walk up the street to the hotel and take a bed for the night. Even as he neared Stolt's livery the urge was strong within him. Natural instinct was for the mind to minimize the threat to Buck and Owen – for the unshaven man was Owen, surely; only he would be tricky enough to shave off his whiskers before riding back to face that tough marshal and his deputy – and leave a man convinced the banker and his cronies, drunk and worn out with arguments raging back and forth, would hold off for the night.

But the sound of the café door crashing open behind him, men noisily emerging, and feet stamping up the plankwalk towards the lights of the saloon had driven all such thoughts from his mind.

84

The danger was here and now. If the cowboy in the café had been talking straight, time was running out. Tom had already consulted his battered turnip watch: with its face tilted to an oil lamp he had seen the finger creeping towards twelve. But that was several long minutes ago. Now the finger would have moved on and would be well into the hour past midnight designated by the cowboy.

He had to hurry. But there was no sense in risking everything against the two armed men in the jail, somehow besting them, only to come tumbling out with Buck and Owen to find the three of them on foot with nowhere to hide. No, before taking that step he had to check on the horses.

Lamplight still glowed in Stolt's window. Tom splashed through the water alongside the streaming walls, could see nothing through the wet, grimy glass, turned into the runway and was immediately in straw-scented gloom.

A crack of light gleamed beneath the office door. Tom knocked with his knuckles. The door swung away from his fist, creaked open. He stepped inside, saw the dirt floor littered with dusty tack, coiled rope hanging from hooks, the smoky lantern suspended over the littered desk. Behind the desk, the chair was empty.

Tom stepped back outside, eased the door shut.

He stood there, straining to listen for signs of human presence in the stables, deliberately shutting out the shouting from higher up the street that put a hard knot of fear in his stomach. But in the livery barn the only sounds were those of horses settled for the night: the rustle of straw, the creak of straining boards as a horse leaned heavily against the side of a stall, a soft, contented snort that brought a fleeting smile to the listener's face.

Stolt, whether compassionate or not, was not on the premises.

Moving like a ghost through the gloom, Tom located his own horse, then Buck's. Owen's was dozing three stalls down, and again Tom allowed himself a smile, this time at his own perception. He had been right: Owen had come back into the Halt after Buck, leaving Adam to make the long ride to Austin.

Their saddles were found just as quickly, hung over a rail. Ten minutes after walking into Stolt's livery, the three horses were roused and saddled. After a moment's thought, Tom moved them back into their stalls. Stolt had settled the animals before he left. He would not check them again.

And now there was nothing more he could do to delay the inevitable confrontation, no more preparation, no more time spent on tasks that were necessary, but done also to waste time because what was to come was scaring him half to death.

But wasting time was putting lives at risk.

Tom wiped his damp palms on his pants, walked back up the runway. He took a deep breath, dropped a hand to his six-gun, stepped out into the rain.

And stopped.

Two men with ducked heads were crossing the street, splashing through wagon ruts streaming with murky water. The man in the heavy mackinaw was Marshal Nat Kimball. The other, wearing a long trailing coat and black hat and with a shiny leather bag banging against his legs, was Doc Howard. They stepped up on to the far plankwalk, kicked mud from their boots and entered the jail.

With a perplexed frown, Tom Lawson eased himself back into the shadows.

'Back up, Lawson, then turn around and stand with your face to the wall.'

'If the doc's about to examine my brother I want—'

'You do as I say, or George Howard stays right where he is.'

Water dripped from Kimball's hat. His tone was unemotional, his eyes cold. The doctor had put down his black bag and was rubbing condensation from the lenses of his spectacles. A small stout man with sharp blue eyes, Owen noted, by his looks mild mannered, making what Buck was about to do that much easier. Owen dismissed him with that cursory glance, looked into Kimball's eyes, hesitated, then backed away, boots scraping on the dirt floor. His heels rattled against the cell's rear wall. He turned, stared fixedly at the damp stone.

There was the soft rasp of a pistol sliding from a leather holster. Keys jingled. A metallic snap was followed by the creak of hinges. Footsteps crossed the cell; others entered, moved to the sides. Out of the corner of his eye Owen saw the moving shadow cast by the oil lamp in the passage. It flowed across the floor, stopped. The doc had reached the bunk, and was bending over Buck.

Owen held his breath. Tension tightened his shoulders. His heart was thundering in his chest.

'Well?'

Kimball, suspecting trickery, already impatient.

'Hold your horses.'

Doc Howard, grumbling, a sawbones not a lawman, not inclined to rush.

Then a sudden flurry of movement, a sharp intake of breath, a sudden taut silence.

'Goddamn!' Jim Folsom said.

'Knew it, I knew it,' Nat Kimball breathed.

'If one of you moves a muscle,' Buck Lawson

said, 'the doc'll be breathin' through a windpipe full of cold steel.'

Owen swung around.

'Get back!' Kimball snapped. 'Your brother's made his play, now you either talk some sense into him or go back to facin' that wall.'

The dim light from the oil lamp washed over the two lawmen, putting the front of Kimball's mackinaw into deep shadow and making a pale blur of his face. They were inside the cell, flanking the open door. Kimball's pistol was cocked and raised, drawing a bead on Owen's throat. Folsom had a Winchester in the crook of his arm, the glinting barrel ready but pointing aimlessly at nothing.

'You listen to me,' Owen Lawson said. 'The only part of this whole crazy business that makes any sense is the fifteen short hours left between us, the judge, and the hang rope. With that in his mind, there's nothing I can do or say to make the kid back off.'

'He's right,' Buck said. 'I'm takin' my chance while there's still time.'

He swung lithely off the bunk, spun Doc Howard and held his left arm in an iron grip as he reached around to bring the blade of the Bowie up beneath the elderly sawbones's chin. The keen edge touched the folds of loose skin. A bead of bright blood glistened.

'All right,' Owen said. 'You lawmen, move. Get

well away from the door, both of you on the same side of the cell, toss your weapons on the bunk. Me and the kid are walking out of here.'

He took two long strides, then a third – and came up against the muzzle of Nat Kimball's pistol as it shifted a fraction and touched his Adam's apple. The lawman was rock steady, his arm high and ramrod straight, his eyes blazing.

'I say we've got a stand-off,' he said quietly, and there was a soft whisper of sound as Doc Howard caught his breath.

Owen grinned savagely.

'Let me tell you something interesting about stand-offs,' he said, and met the marshal's furious gaze with one of mockery. 'The only way they can work is if both parties have got something to lose.'

Tightly, forcing the words from between his teeth, Kimball said, 'I drop this hammer, bits of your backbone hit that wall – and the kid's still there, only now he's on his own.'

'And you've still got the problem of the doc,' Owen said.

'Nat, don't you worry about me,' Howard said. 'This boy has no harm in him.' Unable to move his head because of the knife at his throat, he let his blue eyes glance to either side, narrowed them in chagrin when it seemed that his words had made no impression on the two men locked in confrontation.

'There's no way you can take that knife away from Buck,' Owen told Kimball. 'What you end up with is two dead prisoners, one sawbones with his throat cut.'

'The doc's right, your brother won't do it,' Kimball said, but the eyes that flicked between Owen and the boy with the knife were now unsure. 'You're one-time bank robbers, stole cash for a reason. That reason's been ripped away by a US judge – and it's a long step from theft to cold-blooded murder. Too long.'

'From where I stand right now,' Buck said, 'there's a whole lot more steps to the scaffold, and those are the ones I ain't takin'. Now, you do as the man says, step away from that door, and let me and Owen get the doc out of here in one piece.'

Life and death hung in the balance. Owen felt a surge of pride at Buck's bravado, but heard the words and the boy's shallow, excited breathing as if from a far distance as he locked eyes with the marshal of Boulder Halt. He saw the indomitable will shining in the tough lawman's eyes, sensed his unwillingness to do the unthinkable by backing down; saw also the compassion of the man, the one sterling quality battling with the other as an officer of the law balanced the loss of his prisoners against the certain death of a valued citizen.

Compassion won.

Kimball's arm relaxed. The pistol was pulled back from Owen's throat, the hammer lowered. He stepped away from Owen, nodded to Folsom, and together marshal and deputy walked to the side wall, tossed their weapons on to the cornhusk mattress.

'Yes!' Buck whispered, and there was a tremor in his voice. He nudged Doc Howard. The sawbones moved forwards and Buck went with him, the knife steady at the stout little man's throat. They reached the door, stopped instantly at Owen's sharp command. Owen cast a final glance at the wooden countenance of Nat Kimball, the man's smouldering eyes. Then he brushed past Buck and his hostage, edging sideways so that the lawmen were within his field of vision until he was safely out of the cell.

Turning, he saw that the keys were dangling from the lock.

'All right,' he said. 'Come on through. When you're both clear, I'll lock the cell door.'

Again, Buck pushed Doc Howard, urging him forward. But this time the old man refused to move.

'This is the wrong way to go about it, son,' he said.

'Everything's wrong,' Owen said, 'but playing the hero won't change anything.'

'Move,' Buck said.

'No, I—'

'George, do as he says,' Kimball said.

'Damn you,' George Howard said fiercely, his eyes on Owen.

And the passage door slammed open.

'Hold it right there,' Ed Stolt roared.

Owen spun on his heel, saw the wizened livery man with his face a mask of righteous anger, his harsh words backed up by a cocked scattergun held in hands that shook.

Desperately, seeing the situation slipping out of control, Owen snapped, 'For God's sake drop it, Stolt, or the doc dies!'

But even as he spoke he knew he was too late.

As the passage door slammed open and Owen turned to face the intruder, Nat Kimball sprang like a cougar across the cell. A fist like a big rock was swung wide to slam into the side of Buck's neck. The knife sliced across soft flesh, then fell from nerveless fingers.

Owen heard the crack of knuckles against flesh and bone. Again he turned, this time to see Buck's unconscious body slumping to the dirt floor.

Doc Howard staggered to one side, fingers fumbling at his bloody throat.

'It's over,' Kimball said, and as he dropped into a crouch, the hand that had felled Buck was once again holding his cocked six-gun.

The Robbery at Boulder Halt

Owen shook his head in despair. The scatter-gun's twin muzzles rammed painfully into his back.

Chapter Ten

The big, bearded man brought the horse down the muddy incline with care, knowing that one slip would bring it to its knees, and once down it would be finished. He was a man in the same sorry state of exhaustion as his mount; a man with a gunny-sack lashed behind his saddle, a borrowed hat drooping over sunken black eyes, a rain-saturated duster that had once been white plastered to his bowed frame.

From a short way off, the rocky bluff had been visible through the curtain of rain, a stark, tree-topped landmark after which settlers brought by the advancing railroad had named the town that had become one more halt on the iron horse's crossing of the endless prairie.

But Boulder Halt was still a way off, and Adam Lawson could go no further. Or, he corrected as he swung down in the rock's lee, his horse had done all he had asked of it but was now too wrung-out to carry him. Thirty miles down the line they had gone, into the teeth of the storm; a chance meeting had brought bitter-sweet news; then thirty miles back, the wind abated but the rain incessant, a ride that was always going to be slower than the outward journey and one that had become a waking nightmare for man and beast.

So, for now, this was the end of the road. It was with relief that Adam Lawson made the admission, with a fierce sense of exultation that he off-saddled and fitted his mount with a makeshift hobble, threw saddle, gunny-sack and blanket roll into the shallow dry cave beneath the rock where brittle brushwood provided fuel for a fire.

Later, as he sat by the crackling blaze in his steaming clothes and sipped scalding hot coffee with a cigarette smouldering between his fingers, at the back of his mind there was a mild sense of guilt. But despite the knowledge that their terrible misfortunes could be blamed on Owen, still there was a grudging respect for his older brother, and along with it the firm conviction that everything would be going his way.

Besides which, he comforted himself, if they weren't, then what the hell could he do about it?

Several times as his chilled body soaked up the heat and his eyelids drooped, he snapped awake to gaze back the way he had come, his eyes seeking, ears listening. But he heard nothing, cared even less. He had outpaced them, but not by too much. And he knew now that in any case his forced ride had been futile. His horse was ridden-down, too far gone to be of use until dawn.

By dawn, they would be with him, and that would pose another problem.

But even as he acknowledged the dilemma, prepared to tackle it at once so that he would be one step ahead when they did arrive, his eyelids drooped for the last time.

Adam Lawson slept without awareness, and so exhausted was he that not even the rattle of hooves, the jingle of harness and the ching of spurs – when they came – were enough to rouse him.

Chapter Eleven

The shouting from the jail reached Tom Lawson
only faintly, too faintly for him to distinguish
words, too faintly to reach the ears of the men still
chewing the dog up at the saloon. So he remained
concealed in the livery barn's shadows, skittish as
an untamed bronc, gnawing agitatedly at a
thumbnail, uncertain whether to grab the bull by
the horns and cross the street, or to wait it out,
see what transpired.

In the end, the decision was made for him. The
commotion that seemed to come from the cells at
the back of the jail faded into silence. Seconds
later, two men appeared in the lighted doorway,
stepped down into the mud, started across the
street together.

Doc Howard, accompanied by a gnarled stick of
a man carrying a toolbox and a shotgun. Trying to
hurry, they were sucked back by the mud. They

cursed softly and in unison as, within the space of ten feet, they were drenched by the rain.

'You was lucky,' the gnarled stick said breathlessly. 'More pressure on that blade when Kimball whacked the kid, you'd have been a gonner.'

'The luck turns on your being there repairing the door,' Howard said, puffing and, as he turned his head, Tom Lawson saw a white bandage at his throat. 'I appreciate your timely arrival with that shotgun, and Kimball's swift reaction, but I'm still convinced he was wrong. They were both bluffing. That bluff could have been called at any time, Ed.'

Ed! Tom Lawson sucked in a breath, pressed back into the shadows. So he knew where the compassionate Ed Stolt had gone, what he'd been doing – and where he was now going!

The two men reached the near plankwalk, stepped up, paused while automatically stamping off the caked wet mud.

'Howsomever,' Ed Stolt said, 'what's done is done and Nat's still got his prisoners.'

'But for how much longer?' Howard said, casting a troubled glance towards the lights of the saloon.

'Ain't they all piss and wind?' Stolt queried.

'Maybe, but Frank Warren is a determined man, and he's pushing hard.'

'An' buyin' a few drinks.' Stolt nodded agreement, and turned away. 'Be seein' you, Doc – not too damn soon, I hope, though I reckon it's a faint hope if you're right about the way things are headed.'

He waved a hand, swivelled his head to watch George Howard turn into a side street, then walked quickly out of the wet into the livery stable.

Inside, now well back beyond the projecting bulk of the office, Tom Lawson flattened himself against the stable wall.

He heard the toolbox hit the ground with a crash. Muttering was followed by the slap of a hat as Stolt beat off the water, the groan of hinges, the bang of the office door shutting. A short silence was followed by the scrape of a match. A chair creaked. A man uttered a contented sigh.

Tom Lawson expelled his breath and came silently out of the shadows.

So they'd tried a break, and Buck had been whacked. Stolt's words. But what did they mean? No shot had sounded, so it looked like Kimball had used his fist, or the barrel of a gun. For an instant, Tom bitterly regretted not making his move sooner. If his arrival had coincided with the action started by Owen and Buck, the outcome would have been different. Stolt would have been caught cold from behind. Without the liveryman's shotgun, Kimball would have been helpless. If. . . .

Angrily, Tom shook off the pointless mental pontificating and trod lightly past Stolt's office. He slipped out of the livery barn and moved a short way along the plankwalk, ignoring the water streaming down the walls as he stood back to weigh up the situation.

Up the street, a man had emerged from the saloon and was outlined by the light streaming through the swing doors. Another man joined him, and Tom saw their faces as pale blobs as they turned to look towards the jail.

How much time?

A move now could see him overpower Kimball and Folsom, but trapped in the jail as Warren and his lynch-mob came down the street. Hold back, and he would need to wrest Owen and Buck from the drunken mob. Done that way, he could find the lawmen on his side, but, with the mob defeated, the prisoners would once again be in the hands of the law.

Indecision was muddling Tom's brain as possibilities chased each other like cats after their own tails. He saw a third man emerge from the saloon, caught the glint of several weapons. A glance across at the silent jail revealed nothing more threatening than a closed door, mellow lamplight spilling from the window.

Move. Move now.

But what about the ever present danger posed

by Ed Stolt – a man, according to Doc Howard, who would not stand in his way?

Swiftly, Tom Lawson swung on his heel and went back into the livery barn. Without pause for thought he drew his pistol and barged into the office. Stolt was behind the desk sprawled in the swivel chair, eyes closed in the yellow lamplight as he peacefully smoked his cigarette.

The door crashed against the wall. Stolt's eyes snapped open. Then Tom was on him. He planted one hand on the desk, leaned over and slammed the barrel of his pistol against the old-timer's head. The crack was sickening. Stolt went sideways out of the chair, blood blossoming above his ear.

The shotgun was on the desk. Tom holstered his pistol, grabbed the scattergun, checked the loads and made for the door. He was back on the plankwalk less than thirty seconds after making his decision; halfway across the street before he realized what he was doing and felt fear twist like a knife in his guts and turn his mouth dry.

Yellow mud sucked at his boots. He reached the far plankwalk, stepped up, crossed the slippery boards with two long strides – and stopped.

From up the street, the sound of raised voices.

A pulse was hammering behind his eyes. His lips were drawn back in a grimace, breath hissing through clenched teeth as his chest heaved. He closed his eyes, squeezed them tight enough to cause brilliant flashes of light that became a fading red haze when he again looked at the jail-house door.

Time, time, you're wasting too much goddamn time. . . .

Then he kicked the door open.

He went in as if blown from a cannon, landed with spread legs and with the shotgun cocked and covering the room with its terrible threat. Kimball was behind the desk, mouth comically agape. Folsom was half turned from a file cabinet, hands in a drawer, hair mussed.

'The hell!' Nat Kimball said. 'Twice in one day – and I figured you was still flat on your back.'

Chapter Twelve

The crash of the street door opening shook the building, snapped Owen Lawson's head around.

'Warren,' he said, and rose tensely to his feet. 'They finally got the guts to make a move.'

Buck shook his head, and winced. 'My neck's already broke. Let 'em hang me, put me out of my misery.'

Owen's grin was savage.

'I'd like to oblige, but it ain't over. Kimball won't give up easy. And if that mob does drag us out of here, it's still some ways to a tall tree strong enough for both of us.'

With his ears tuned to what was going on he watched Buck absently, pale-faced, hand massaging his bruised neck, then whirled like a cat to face the passage as voices were raised.

'You hear that?' he said softly, and when he turned to his brother a light shone in his eyes.

'Tom?' Buck said, alert now and frowning. 'Jesus, Owen, I saw him go down outside the bank, take a slug in the guts, there—'

He broke off, watching Owen as footsteps approached the door.

'Down,' Owen said, and Buck flattened himself on the bunk.

Owen stepped to the side of the cell, close to the bars, put his back to the wall . . . waited.

The first man through was a glowering Nat Kimball; the first thing Owen noticed was the absence of a gunbelt. He was followed by Jim Folsom, also looking peeved and peculiarly naked without a pistol at his hip. Then came a wan looking Tom Lawson, and Owen's face broke into a wide grin.

'Boy, are you a sight for tired eyes.'

'Later, Owen.' Tom Lawson shook his head, glared ferociously at the two lawmen, said, 'Back off,' and waggled the shotgun.

'Easy,' Kimball said soothingly, 'that damn thing's cocked.'

With both lawmen backed out of the way Tom stepped forward and hurriedly unlocked the cell. Buck rolled off the bunk, came upright with a final shake to clear his head. Owen moved away from the wall and was swiftly out of the cell and making for the office.

'Tom, Buck, get them inside the cell, lock them

in. Make sure they stay quiet. I'll get the guns.'

The words were flung over his shoulder as he went through the door into the fuggy office, snatched their two gunbelts off wall hooks, located Buck's Winchester and, after a moment's thought, gathered two more rifles from the rack and as many boxes of shells as he could carry.

Then, arms loaded, he called, 'Right, leave them, let's move out!' and crossed to the street door that Tom had thoughtfully left ajar.

He was easing it open with his foot when Tom and Buck came tumbling out of the passage, cautiously poking his head out when Buck took his gunbelt, buckled it on and relieved Owen of his gleaming Winchester.

'Put these in your pockets.'

Owen handed out the shells, passed a Winchester to Tom who hesitated, then left Stolt's shotgun on the desk.

'Tom,' Owen said, again looking up the street, 'I guess you know something of what's going on. Could you see what was happening at the saloon?'

'Enough to know we're wastin' time talkin'.'

'Yeah,' Owen said, and pulled his head in. 'As of this minute we're plumb out of time. Warren and his mob are halfway down the street. If we go out, we go out fast, make for Stolt's.'

'Horses are saddled and ready.'

'The livery's back doors open?'

Tom swore. 'I didn't check.'

'No matter. First, somehow, we've got to make it across the street.'

'What about one at a time?' Buck said, 'the others layin' down coverin' fire?'

'Good thinking, but too late,' Owen said. 'They're damn near on us, if—'

'Shut the door,' Tom said, and grinned as Owen flashed him a puzzled glance. 'Hell, why go out the front and face a drunken mob when this place has got a back door?'

'Goddamn!'

Owen stepped back, kicked the door shut and slammed the timber bar into its brackets. Buck was already out of the office and, as Owen followed Tom, he heard the rattle of a lock, a sudden blast of cold air on his face.

He ran past the cells, conscious of the silent, watchful lawmen. Blackness waited beyond the open back door and, as he stepped out into the drenching rain and dragged the door shut, he was momentarily blinded. Then his eyes adjusted. The blackness became the murky grey of falling rain and the walls of crumbling shacks ranging along the far side of the narrow alley that ran parallel to the main street, the light a faint reflection on the glistening walls.

'Over here,' Tom whispered.

They were ten feet away, tight up against the

back wall of the jail. Beyond them, light washed across the dirt from an intersecting alley that led to the street.

'They'll be almost on the jail,' Tom said tightly. 'They get inside, Kimball will point the way. Then they'll come pilin' out that back door.'

'Only we won't be here,' Buck said cheerfully.

'Damn right,' Owen said. 'We move while they're crashing around in there. Only chance we've got. But you, Tom – you OK?'

'I made it this far, I'll make it all the way.'

'Good man!'

He splashed past them, glanced swiftly down the intersecting alley then beckoned them forwards. As they turned the corner and walked rapidly down the side of the jail towards the lamplight, a sudden, explosive volley of oaths reached their ears, followed by yells of fury, the slam of doors, the pounding of boots.

'Jesus, that was quick!' Tom growled.

'So we'll be quicker,' Owen said.

'You bet,' Buck said, 'only I've got me a real bad feeling.'

And then they reached the street.

At once, a rifle cracked.

Splinters of wood flew from the nearby hitch rail. A second shot thumped into the jail's wall. A third kicked up wet dirt between Owen's boots as he leaped back and flattened himself against the wall.

'There's a man posted in the livery, maybe Stolt backing him,' he said, and stared into his brothers' haunted faces.

Behind them, they could hear the mob piling out of the jail's back door to splash noisily along the alley.

Chapter Thirteen

'A couple of men at a distance are easier to face than half-a-dozen close up,' Owen said, thinking fast. 'Buck, you were right. I'll cover you and Tom, you do the same for me when you're both across the street.'

'It won't work, they're too close.'

'Move, Tom, now!'

He gave his tall, bearded brother a hard shove in the back and, through the curtain of rain, watched him duck his head and splash after Buck through thick mud and wagon ruts running with water. Then, desperate to get clear of the approaching mob, Owen stepped around the corner, leaped up on to the slick plankwalk on the opposite side of the alley from the jail and half fell into a doorway.

Buck and Tom were already halfway across the street, snapping fast, running shots at the livery barn with their pistols. For a moment, the guns inside were shocked into silence. Then, as the two men back in the shadows beyond the big double doors recovered and rifles began to spit flame, Owen jacked a shell into his Winchester and began to lay down a rapid covering fire. He worked the lever fast, planting a line of bullets along the inside of the barn's wide opening. And all the time, above the crack of his own rifle and the rattle of pistols, he could hear the angry bellows of the men pounding around from behind the jail.

Beaten back by his accurate fire, the men in the barn were again forced to stop firing. And now Buck and Tom had made it across the street. Buck leaped up into the shelter of the mercantile's stoop, crossed it and ducked down behind a stack of heavy barrels. Tom ran twenty yards, kicked open the door of Annie's Café with a crackle of splintering frame and vanished into the gloom.

'Owen!' he yelled. 'Move yourself!'

Then the mob from the jail reached the street. A bulky figure appeared at the corner of the alley. At close range, Owen snapped a shot. Splinters flew. The man roared, brought his pistol around then fell back with a yell of fright as Owen's second shot clipped his ear and his shoulder was spattered with blood. Those rushing up from behind flung him forward. He landed on his knees in the mud, scrambled for the plankwalk in front of the jail. Unbalanced, the two men who had pushed him lurched from the alley and were met by a withering crossfire as Tom and Buck began to use their rifles.

Seizing the chance to join his brothers, Owen moved out of the doorway and strode across the plankwalk. But now, with Tom and Buck occupied in driving back the mob and Owen's rifle silent, the men in the barn rejoined the fray. Two rifles opened up. Slugs hissed and whined around Owen, plucked at his sleeves, sliced across his shoulder like a red-hot knife blade. As he frantically back-pedalled, an ankle turned, a boot slipped. He fell, landed heavily on his back, rolled as a bullet kicked splinters into his face. Jarred loose, the Winchester flew from his hand, plopped into the mud and sank. Still rolling for his life, he crashed against the wall, climbed to his feet, cast a swift glance about him.

Over at the mercantile, safe behind the heavy barrels, Buck had cleverly switched his rifle's fire to the barn and was again driving the two men back. From the comparative safety of the café, Tom was carefully picking his shots to keep the mob in the alley occupied: in its narrow, open mouth, without cover, they were dangerously exposed.

The street was clear, the opposition silenced.

But it would be only scant moments, Owen knew, before some bright spark used his head and the mob ran back the way it had come and split up. The alley running parallel to the main street would allow them to outflank the Lawsons without being seen: using alleys intersecting the buildings to the east and west, the two groups would emerge on the main street and begin a pincer movement with the Lawsons trapped in the jaws. With one man left to guard the alley and two men across the street in the livery barn, there would be nowhere for the Lawsons to run, or hide.

Then, as the impossibility of their situation began to sink in, Owen was shocked to hear a rifle open up from the saloon, and again ducked back into his doorway as the newcomer's volley was echoed shot for shot by the rifles in the livery barn.

As if to mock him with the accuracy of his prediction, a single shot banged from the alley. As its echoes died away, he heard the splash of boots through the pools of rainwater in the alley as a number of men retreated.

The mercantile was silent, though lamplight glowed in the alley running alongside it from a window in a side wall. If Annie was awake in her rooms at the rear of the café, she would keep her head down as long as Tom remained on the premises.

To the east, across from the saloon, a light appeared in one of the hotel's downstairs windows. A door opened a crack and a woman's voice called out.

The crackle of gunfire died into an uneasy silence.

'Tom!' Owen bawled.

'I hear you!'

'Buck?'

'Yeah?'

'They're working to come at us from both ends of the street.'

'So what now?'

This was Tom, and Owen realized that, out of jail, the responsibility for the family was again his. Well, so be it. He had got them in, now he had to get them out. But how? Stay on the street and fight a desperate running battle? Keep separated, or regroup? Either way, their aim must be to reach the horses – but even with all the other threats removed, it would be impossible to dislodge Stolt and his *compadre*. With a single door back and front, two men could hold the big barn against an army, and with armed men bearing down on them from all directions the Lawsons had no time for a siege.

So if they couldn't make the barn, if it was impossible to get to the horses. . . ?

Time was running out. The mob was moving

fast to new positions on the flanks that would seal both ends of town, but were out of earshot. The man guarding the alley was close, but keeping his head down. Stolt and his sidekick had stopped shooting, but were sure to be watchful and alert. Alert, because they knew damn well what the Lawsons needed if they were to get clear of Boulder Halt.

So, Owen decided with a surge of excitement, let's play along with them.

Deliberately pitching his voice loud and clear, he called, 'Tom, we need those horses fast. Cover me, I'm coming across.'

Without waiting for a reply he pushed himself away from the wall, crossed the plankwalk in three long strides and leaped down into the mud. He sank to his ankles, kicked against a hard object and knew he'd found his Winchester, cursed softly as he left it where it was and ploughed on. He was halfway across before the first rifle opened up from the barn; three-quarters of the way before the second sent a slug whining past his ear.

Ducking and weaving as best he could in the thick ooze, he saw Buck step out from behind the stacked barrels and trigger three fast shots at the barn.

'Buck, leave them!' he yelled. 'Go join Tom.'

Panting, he slipped, went down on one knee in

the morass and felt the wind of a bullet pass through the space above his head. As he rose from the clinging mud, he saw Buck spring from the stoop and race towards the café. Then Owen was across. They came together in front of the splintered door, leaped inside, stood in the darkness sucking in great gulps of stale, greasy air.

'Is there a back way out?' Owen gasped.

'I guess,' Tom said, moving to touch his elbow, 'but going for the barn's a crazy idea.'

'We're not.'

'But you said,' Buck blurted.

'So let them think it.'

Quicker on the uptake, Tom chuckled. 'So – where, then, Owen?'

'To hole up for a spell in just about the biggest place in town,' Owen said, and moved away to thread his way between the tables.

Crowding him, anxious to get out, Buck said, 'Only places I know're the bank, the saloon across the way, but the bank's locked and that feller Flanagan's out front takin' pot shots.'

'I think he's talkin' about the hotel,' Tom said.

'Right,' Owen said. 'We move in fast and without a disturbance we can be in there a while before they figure out where we've gone.'

He cast a swift glance back at the open front door then led the way through the kitchen to another interior door. When he opened it and

116

continued on through they were in a gloomy lit living-room containing bed, chiffonier, and a couple of chairs placed at a plain wooden table. Annie was in the bed, dark hair mussed. She scrambled backwards until she was up against the headboard, covers clutched to her chin.

Owen said, 'Beg pardon, ma'am,' tipped his hat, then made quickly for the back door. As he opened it he heard his brothers muttering their apologies. Then once again he was out in a narrow, dismal alley identical to all the others. The smell of decay was in his nostrils. He was being drenched by the unrelenting downpour, with the lights of the main street reflecting on crumbling timber walls and the soggy earth.

The door clicked shut.

'Goddamn rain,' Buck said, and laughed nervously.

'Owen, there's blood on your shirt.'

He remembered the feel of a hot knife slicing flesh, touched his shoulder, took his fingers away sticky with blood.

'A scratch,' he told Tom. 'But what about you? Both of us saw Kimball trigger a shot, you go down outside the bank.'

'Bruised ribs is all. I'll live, we all will.'

'I guess we're all a mite frayed around the edges.'

'And more to come before this is over,' Tom said grimly.

117

Owen nodded. 'The hotel's immediately after the bank,' he said, listening to distant sounds of menace. 'The blonde woman who owns it's awake, I heard her shout across to that saloonist.'

'We go in the back way,' Tom said, 'she'll shoot out the front like a frightened rabbit. That puts paid to your hope of goin' unnoticed.'

'And just about now the half of that mob that headed for this end of town will be coming out of the alley across the road – the one that runs alongside Flanagan's.'

'Which makes it nigh on impossible for one of us to go round the front, stop her leavin'.' Tom shook his head.

'Nah!' Buck's voice was scornful. 'The fellers in the barn, the one they left in the alley – hell, Owen, all three of 'em all heard what you shouted.'

'Yeah, that's right. They figure we went through that alley so's we could get near the horses.' Owen nodded. 'The mob will get the word, head fast down the street towards Stolt's livery barn – and I reckon Flanagan will go with them.'

He clapped Buck on the shoulder, then turned to splash his way up the alley. The back windows of the bank were barred. Beyond it, on the other side of the intersecting alley, the high bulk of the hotel loomed against the weeping night skies. Wooden steps led up to a back door. Light shone palely through a curtained window.

'We make some noise goin' in,' Owen said softly, looking along the alley to the street, 'she'll rush for the front door. You two wait here. As soon as that mob's moved down the street, I'll give the signal. When I do, kick that back door open. If we play it right, she'll run straight into my arms.'

He left them. The alley he was in was directly opposite the one running alongside the saloon. He made for the street, hugging the wall. As he reached it, figures exploded from the opposite alley, drawn pistols glinting in the wan light: he recognized the red-haired wag he had seen in the saloon, his mournful companion, the cowboy who, in the light of a wet dawn, had crossed the street to the livery – hell, what seemed days ago but was only a matter of some eighteen hours.

Then, from down the street, a voice rang out.

'They're after the horses!'

Ed Stolt.

At once, the three men making up this section of the lynch mob swung away from the alley and began pounding down the plankwalk. At a slower pace, the bearded figure of Sean Flanagan left the saloon to follow them, rifle discarded, his favoured shotgun held loose at his side.

Owen Lawson turned, lifted a hand, then slipped out of the alley.

He kept tight up against the front of the hotel,

crossed the lighted window he had seen from further down the street, reached the door he had seen opened.

It was now closed.

As he reached it, faintly to his ears there came the sound of timber splintering.

Chapter Fourteen

How far does the sound of gunfire travel? How close to those of wild beasts are a man's instincts?

As Adam Lawson's eyes snapped open and he rolled, shivering, off the bed of dry brushwood, those questions passed through his mind but remained unanswered. He could hear nothing but the steady beat of the falling rain, sense even less. Yet something had dragged him from an exhausted sleep, snapped him wide awake as surely as if a pistol had been fired close to his ear.

The fire was a bed of grey embers, a dim glow at their heart. The land sloping up from the hollow in the cliff face was a deserted expanse of soaking wet leaves and brush at the far side of which his hobbled horse dozed under the trees.

So, still no sign of them.

He climbed to his feet, scratching, yawned, looked with longing at the remains of the fire, at the dry brushwood that would bring it flaring and crackling to light and warmth.

Then he shut his mind to all thoughts of comfort, rolled a cigarette, and turned instead to contemplation of what lay ahead in the town of Boulder Halt.

'You know what you've got to do,' Owen had said.

'I know,' Adam had replied.

He had agreed because he had thought what was demanded of him by his older brother to be so far in the realms of fantasy that his loyalty would never be put to the test. Well, a few short hours was all it had taken to show how wrong he was. The test was upon him – so, how strong was his allegiance to the family? Should blood-ties be allowed to overrule common sense?

Angrily, he blew smoke.

Harsh words had been spoken after their escape from town. But his opposition to Owen's wild ideas that had brought them south to the bank robbery in Boulder Creek had always been open and, in the end, he had been proved right: they were cowmen, not thieves, and they had bungled the job.

But with one brother dead and another in jail, he had found it impossible to do the sensible thing and return home licking his wounds. Despite losing half their numbers and leaving town in a hail of lead, they had got the cash they needed. So, he had ridden down the line to another lost cause, ridden back again bearing the added weight of a promise that must be honoured. For, when everything had been done and said, won and lost – he was a Lawson.

'Yeah, I know what to do,' he had said.

And he did.

Adam Lawson flicked away the cigar, watched it arc away through the rain, then reached for his saddle.

Chapter Fifteen

Her breath was hot against his skin, the musk perfume of her hair in his nostrils as he clamped his hand across her mouth, used his left arm around her waist to pull her in close. Above his fingers her blue eyes were wide, but in them there was not terror, but contempt.

She moaned softly as he pushed her back into the hallway and kicked the door closed with his heel. At once they were in soft, warm light, the lamplight he had seen through the window but which now washed into the hallway from the open door of the front room.

He could hear footsteps at the rear of the building, drawing closer; saw, from her eyes, that she was aware of them, had been driven by fear of them to rush to the front door. Other noises could be heard faintly through the solid street door:

distant voices, the faint pop of a single shot, sudden, confused shouting.

He had walked out of the alley and she had run straight into his arms.

'I'll take my hand away,' Owen said, 'if you'll promise to keep quiet.'

'Mmb, mmb.' Her eyes narrowed, and she tried to nod.

'Yes or no.' He smiled crookedly. 'Blink once for yes. I'll trust you.'

There was a pause. Then, quite clearly, she blinked once.

Owen took his hand away.

At the far end of the hallway, Tom appeared, closely followed by a wide-eyed Buck.

'Bank robbers,' the blonde woman said and, as she dragged the back of her hand across her mouth, her tone was withering. 'And you'll trust *me*!'

'At risk to our safety, I trusted you not to cry out,' Owen said. 'You've nothing to fear from us.'

'Damn right,' she said, and swiftly loosed herself from Owen's grasp. 'You've already stepped on Frank's toes. He finds out about this—'

'You must be Laura Beckett,' Tom said. He caught Owen's swift glance, shrugged, said, 'Her and Warren're gettin' hitched, I heard talk over at the doc's, in Annie's.'

'I ain't never in my life,' Buck said, 'seen a place as rich-lookin' as this!'

'Then let's hope it don't get too badly smashed up,' Owen said, watching the woman. 'You and Warren may be getting married, ma'am, but plying those men with hard liquor was like throwing kerosene on a fire.'

'They'll follow his orders,' she said, her lip curling.

'But in any case,' Tom said, 'from what you say we've now got ourselves a mighty valuable bargainin' chip.'

'Oh, no,' she said, shaking her head. 'Your big brother just told me I had nothing to fear.'

'And it's true, but Frank Warren doesn't know that,' Owen cut in grimly. 'Buck, Tom, secure the doors, back and front. Ma'am, let's you and me go upstairs.'

'No—'

'All we want is a room overlooking the street.'

'You can have every damn room in the place, just let me go.'

'Right now, nobody knows where we are or what we're doing. The minute you walk out of here—'

'I won't say anything—'

'Is it a habit of yours to walk the streets after midnight in the pouring rain?'

She looked at him dumbly. Gently, he touched her arm. She jerked back, turned and walked stiffly away.

'Before that, put out the lights,' Owen said.

'You've called across the street to Flanagan, wished him goodnight, stepped back inside. Now you're going to bed.'

They waited. She went into the front room. The soft sound of breath being expelled was followed by darkness, the smell of the hot wick. She was an indistinct shadow when she emerged. They watched her walk along the passage, hitch her long skirts daintily and climb the stairs.

'The doors,' Owen repeated to Tom and Buck. 'When that's done, come on up.'

The stair carpets were worn but clean and, as he followed Laura Beckett, Owen found himself agreeing with Buck's assessment. This was no ordinary, run-down frontier hotel, and he was filled with admiration for the woman who had stamped the establishment with her personality and her standards, then maintained them despite the daily abuse of the facilities by travellers and cow hands accustomed to spittoons, bare boards and cornhusk mattresses.

Right now the place appeared to be empty of guests, and he breathed a prayer of thankfulness before taking the last few stairs at a run as the shouting in the street increased, and drew nearer.

The landing doubled back. One door was open. Inside the room, weak light filtering through parted curtains revealed Laura Beckett perched on a straight-backed chair, her face amused.

'They're coming up the street. So much for their not knowing.'

'No, they're hunting blind,' Owen said. 'They've lost us, think maybe we've left town on foot.'

'But you've barred the doors. If they knock, I won't answer. They'll know at once something is wrong, and the only thing wrong with this town is you, Mr—'

'Lawson,' Owen said, and shook his head. 'I told you. You spoke to Flanagan, came in and shut the door. He saw that. If they're heading this way, they'll have seen the light doused. If Warren's got any thought for you, he'll let you sleep.'

'My marrying the man doesn't make him a saint, or a fool. He'll hammer on that door until he gets an answer.'

'The only answer he'll get,' Tom Lawson said, 'is a bullet.'

The faint light glistened on the two rifles as Tom and Buck crowded into the room. Tom crossed to the window, stepped carefully to one side and twitched the curtain back with the rifle. Buck sat on the bed, took a carton of .44-40 shells from his pocket and began to reload his '73 Winchester.

'They're on to us,' Tom murmured.

And the woman jumped with shock as someone hammered hard on the front door with a rifle butt.

'Laura! You all right in there?'

'That's Frank,' she said, white-faced.

'She could poke her head out the window,' Buck said, 'tell him everything's dandy.'

Owen glanced at her, met her defiant gaze and shook his head.

'We wait.'

The hammering went on, interspersed with Warren's increasingly hoarse shouts, short periods of silence.

'They're talkin',' Tom said, and turned from the window. 'I guess those men out there expect you to answer your fiancé, ma'am. You ain't done it, so what they're sayin' is your man should break down the door.'

'Drive them back,' Owen said tightly, and Laura Beckett moaned softly.

With a swift jab, Tom shattered the window. There was a sudden outcry as shards of glass showered the mob at the door. Buck swiftly crossed the room. Tom poked his rifle out, angled the barrel downwards and triggered a shot. Then Buck was at the other side of the window. Shouts of panic were followed by the splashing of mud as men hastily crossed the street or ran into the alleys. Buck blazed three fast shots. Across the street, glass shattered in the saloon.

Then the mob opened up with rifles and pistols. A volley of shots ripped the curtains to shreds, pocked the walls with black holes. The remaining glass was plucked from the window frame. Glistening splinters spattered the carpet, peppered the walls, stung Owen's cheek.

'Ma'am, get down!' Owen roared and, as she remained frozen with fright and hot lead swept the room, he dropped to the floor, swung his leg wide and kicked the chair out from under her.

She landed on her rump, squealed with indignation.

On either side of the window, Tom and Buck were flattened against the wall. Owen snaked over to them, climbed to his feet.

Above the deafening gunfire he said, 'They got any sense at all, they'll be using covering fire the way we did.'

'I drove two or three into the alley,' Tom said.

'So they'll go for the back door,' Buck said.

Even as he spoke, there was a lull in the shooting and they could hear thunderous blows at the rear of the hotel. With a gusting cry of relief, Laura Beckett scrambled up off the floor and dashed from the room in a flurry of skirts.

'Go after her, both of you,' Owen snapped. 'Buck, you grab her. Tom, that door ain't strong enough to stand too much pounding, or thick enough to stop a slug. Get there fast, give them a taste of hot lead.'

He heard them tumble down the stairs, the

sudden desperate cry of the woman in the downstairs passage followed by the muffled thump of
Tom's rifle.

Where was Kimball?

Thinking back as he crossed to the window and
looked out with the cold night air and the smell of
rain in his face, Owen knew that the mob had not
lingered to free the two lawmen. Kimball and
Folsom were still in the cell. But if they weren't,
would it make any difference?

'Warren!'

'I hear you.'

'Go get the marshal.'

'No sir. You throw down your guns and walk
out, or we get torches and burn the place down
around your ears.'

'You know your woman's in here?'

'I do.'

'And that makes no difference?'

Soft footsteps coming into the room. Heavier
ones behind. Gunsmoke strong and acrid. The
catch of a woman's breath, the musk scent of her
perfume.'

'What happens to her is no longer my responsibility, Lawson.'

'Or maybe never has been, or ever will be?'
Owen suggested, and heard the woman's soft gasp
of anger.

'She lives or dies,' Warren said without concern,

'one way or another you're coming out.'

Then another voice chipped in, low and hard, the words indistinct but bringing a sharp reply from Warren. Owen looked away from the window, frowning, saw Laura Beckett held firm by Buck and gazed into her stricken blue eyes.

'That was Sean Flanagan,' she said. 'If I'm at risk, he'll argue with Frank.'

'Bring in the law?'

'I don't know. But he'll talk sense.'

A glimmer of hope? But with Warren crazy for revenge, the men drunk and without the restraints of the law, was it enough?

Turning again to the window, Owen called, 'What about this for an alternative? You and your men back off as far as the jail. Send Stolt up with the horses. Then give us the length of the street and we'll take our chance.'

The offer was met by a barking laugh. 'What I've sent for,' Warren said, 'is rags and coal oil. You've got thirty seconds, then the whole place goes up in flames.'

Chapter Sixteen

The freshening breeze was in Adam Lawson's face as he rode into Boulder Halt, the promise of drier weather to come in its soft warmth and the perceptible lightening of the night skies.

But the mild air that was drawing the deep chill from his bones carried with it the stink of gunsmoke that set his nerves on edge, making him fearful for his brothers' safety. That fear became like an insistent, nagging toothache when he squinted through the rain and saw, at the far end of town, figures lurking in the shadows on the plankwalk fronting the saloon and at the mouth of the alley by the hotel. Weapons glinted. Harsh voices were carried by the moist breeze, raised in anger.

One man was out in the middle of the street, his voice a fierce bark of authority, a no-nonsense tone accustomed to getting its way. A big man

with a rifle loose in his hands, a man who was
oblivious to the downpour as he yelled up at one
of the hotel's upper windows.

As Adam rode towards Stolt's Livery and Feed
and the jail, a skinny man with a lined face
emerged from the stables' open doors, stepped
down into the mud and, with his head twisted to
watch the action at the top end of town, began to
splash across the street.

Ed Stolt, Adam decided, glancing back at the
name over the doors. Heading for the jail and
keeping a keen eye on the fracas, which suggested
that what was going on up the street was not the
marshal's doing. But if it wasn't, why was Kimball
inside his office letting all hell break loose?

If Buck was in a cell, could be Kimball was
protecting his prisoner. But from what? A lynch-
mob would be clamouring outside the jail. This
mob was at the far end of town, swarming around
the hotel. They were baying for blood – but whose
blood? Owen's? Had he hung around for most of
the day, made his play in darkness and got
himself cornered?

Still musing with considerable trepidation on
the imponderable, Adam held his horse back until
Stolt had passed, watching the wiry figure fight to
stay on his feet as he negotiated the slick mud
then stepped up on to the far plankwalk and
stamped noisily into the jail.

Then, using the rain as an excuse to tug his hat brim down low and tuck his head into his chest so that his bearded face was swallowed up in dark shadows, he gently nudged the tired horse forward and walked it at an angle across the street so that he could make his way up town under cover of the buildings' looming false fronts.

As he drew nearer to the hotel, he could see that in one window on the first floor the glass was shattered, the curtains torn. Then, somewhere in the hotel, a woman cried out, the shrill cry followed by two muffled shots. Moments later two men emerged at a run from the alley alongside the hotel. A signal passed between them and the man in the street. He turned, gestured with the rifle. And some way down the street, level with Adam, two more men came out of a doorway and began stumbling up the plank walk carrying a heavy metal drum.

Then, as Adam drew rein some twenty yards down the street from the saloon, dismounted and threw a quick hitch over the nearest rail, a voice he recognized rang out clear and loud from the upstairs room.

'Warren!'

'I hear you.'

The big man. Barking his reply. Out in the middle of the street, ankle deep in mud. Frank Warren, then. The owner of the bank, fighting hard for his cash.

135

'Go get the marshal.'

'No sir. You throw down your guns and walk out, or we get torches and burn the place down around your ears.'

'You know your woman's in here?'

'I do.'

'And that makes no difference?'

'What happens to her is no longer my responsibility, Lawson.'

'Or maybe never has been, or ever will be?'

'She lives or dies,' Warren said without concern, 'one way or another you're coming out.'

Adam stepped up on to the plankwalk. He hugged the wall, walking in shadows, caught the glow of a cigarette, the murmur of voices. The men he could see as indistinct shapes had their weapons drawn. Adam grinned, slipped out his pistol, held it high and cocked it noisily.

Close by, a man's eyes glinted wetly as he turned his head.

'Wait,' he said. 'Warren'll give the word.'

Like hell he will, Adam thought.

Out in the street, a lean man with a red beard had moved alongside the banker. Angry words were exchanged, then the bearded man swung around and splashed back towards the saloon. The man who had spoken to Adam spat disgustedly.

'Ain't no secret Flanagan fancies the woman,'

he said, loud enough for his voice to travel. 'But for Warren there ain't nothing can replace the money them fellers took.'

'Glad to hear it,' Adam said softly, and felt rather than saw the man's suspicious look. Suddenly the air was alive with tension. Boots scraped as the man moved closer. Adam half turned, bracing himself.

'What about this for an alternative?'

Owen, shouting down again, and Adam let his breath out softly as the suspicious character stopped and looked up at the window. And now Adam could see Owen, off to one side, half hidden by the ripped curtains.

'You and your men back off as far as the jail,' Owen called. 'Send Stolt up with the horses. Then give us the length of the street and we'll take our chance.'

Warren laughed. 'What I've sent for,' he said, 'is rags and coal oil. You've got one minute, then the whole place goes up in flames.'

And at his words the two men who had hurried up the plankwalk banged the drum down in the alley. Liquid sloshed. The stink of coal oil was heavy on the air as the inflammable liquid was splashed on the hotel's timber walls.

'Hurry along there,' Warren barked. Then, 'You up there, Lawson – you've got thirty seconds!'

The empty drum hit the ground and rolled

hollowly. A match flared. The ends of torches crudely fashioned from branches and rags were dipped in the coal oil, and lighted. The street was illuminated by their smoking flames.

'Hold it right there!'

Adam stepped out of the shadows, moved to the edge of the plankwalk and jumped down into the mud.

Warren turned his head.

'Feller, you stay out of this. If you ain't got the stomach for it, get the hell out of here.'

'I did,' Adam said. 'After I robbed the bank. But then I came back.'

And as Frank Warren spun to face him he lifted his head and let the banker see his full, dark beard.

Chapter
Seventeen

'He means business.'

Owen let the curtain fall, stepped away from the window and flung a withering glance at Tom.

'Hell, so do we.'

'Yeah,' Buck said, listening apprehensively at the window, 'but I can already hear them splashin' coal oil. We don't move now, it'll be too—'

'You up there, Lawson – you've got thirty seconds!'

At the harsh bark of Warren's voice, Laura Beckett said desperately, 'This is my hotel, I can't believe he'd burn it down.'

Owen looked at Buck.

'I heard that splashin', the clatter of an empty drum – then it went quiet.'

'He'll do it,' Owen said grimly.

'Then we've got no choice, and no time left,' Tom said.

'Down the stairs, everybody.'

Owen waited until they were out of the room, then followed, urging them on as they hastily descended to the ground floor.

'Make for the back,' he called. 'They've tasted hot lead once, they'll stay clear.'

By the time he had caught up with them, Tom had slammed back the big iron bolts at the top and bottom of the bullet-riddled back door. When he eased it open, the cool draught brought in the scent of rain, the heady taste of freedom.

The alley running parallel to the main street was empty. Tom and Buck passed him, rifles glinting as they headed away into the darkness at a jog. Alone with the woman, Owen poked his head around the corner and looked along the intersecting alley towards main street. Two men. An empty oil drum. The lamplight from the saloon glinting on the timber walls of the hotel that were soaked by something more sinister than the incessant rain.

But the men were standing still, looking towards the street.

Someone was talking.

It was a voice he recognized.

'You know where my brothers have gone,' Owen said, turning to Laura Beckett. 'We need our horses, so they've headed for Stolt's.' He looked into her blue eyes, put kindness into his smile.

'You go to Warren, tell him we're out, tell him there's no need to burn down your hotel.'

'You're letting me go?'

'A hostage gave us one way out, but now there's another.'

She frowned, her eyes searching his face. 'All right. And thank you. I'll tell him that you're out of the hotel, but no more,' she said, her chin lifted, 'because even that's more than he deserves.'

Owen shook his head, and touched her arm. 'Don't think too harshly of him. We've given him and his daughter a hard time, and this dirty work was a carefully calculated risk. I'm sure he knew you'd walk out before things got out of control.'

He put pressure on his hand, turned her so that she was facing the main street, watched her walk along the alley. Her hair was a gold veil against the light; her long skirt brushed the slick mud. Beyond her, a man could be seen, a tall man with a dark beard, wearing a hat that Owen had last seen when he removed it from his own head as the wind and rain tore at the exposed bluff to the east of Boulder Halt.

A sense of exultation swept over him as three men crossed the end of the alley, coming from the lower end of town: Kimball, Folsom and Stolt. So now there was a clear way out, a better, honourable way out. Adam had returned with the offer of a trade-off that couldn't be refused. The

town marshal and his deputy were there to see
fair play.

He hesitated for a moment longer, watched the
woman reach the end of the alley as the men came
together in the middle of the street. Then he
turned and quickly made his way to Stolt's.

In the cool fresh darkness of the stables the
sound and the smell of horses set his heart pounding. Tom and Buck were already in the saddle,
Winchesters in saddle boots, Tom holding the
reins of the third horse. Owen took them, found a
stirrup and swung over leather, turned the horse
towards the barn's big doors.

'No, Owen,' Buck said, and his voice was tight
with excitement. 'They're up the far end of town.
We go out the back way, head west down the alley,
we can be gone before they know it.'

'We go out the front,' Owen said, savouring the
moment. 'We're going back up town.'

'The hell!' Tom said. 'You gone crazy?'

'Adam's talking to them,' Owen said, and
showed his teeth in a broad grin.

It knocked them speechless. A horse moved,
snorting, and Tom automatically stilled it with his
hand. Buck was staring open-mouthed at Owen.

'You knew,' Tom said.

'I knew he'd come, but not when,' Owen said.

'What about Ike?'

'Ike's dead.'

142

Tom swore. 'So everything we've gone through was for nothing.'

'Yeah, but hindsight comes too late to be of any help at the outset.'

After a moment Tom nodded slowly. 'You think they'll go for it?'

Buck was watching him with a puzzled frown. 'Go for what?'

'If we don't need the cash,' Tom said, 'I guess we're about to use it to buy freedom.'

'I guess we are,' Owen said.

'If we stay alive long enough.'

'There is that,' Owen said, and with an encouraging wink at Buck he nudged his horse towards the doors.

They rode up the street in much the same way that Tom, Adam and Buck had ridden in before the bank robbery: three brothers abreast in the centre of the road, riding through the mud and the swirling rain towards Boulder Halt's bank. But this time they were not riding out of the dawn into a sleepy, unsuspecting town where the shock of a surprise raid would put the gods firmly on their side; now they were heading for a showdown where the cards were stacked against them and the dealer dealt in death. Frank Warren was as likely to meet them with a hail of bullets as with an ear tuned to the logic of their words; more likely, Owen thought with deep misgivings, for there could surely be no reasoning with a man who, for the sake of a few dollars and his own damaged pride, would willingly burn down the building in which his betrothed was being held hostage?

But reason with him they must, if they were to leave Boulder Halt any way other than in a pine box.

The road ahead was empty, but lamps had been lit by Laura Beckett to bring warmth and life back to the hotel and, across the street, a flood of lamplight poured from the windows of Flanagan's place. To Owen Lawson it seemed that the town's saloon was forever to be the scene of argument and obstinacy, of cantankerousness tinged with wry humour, for along with the lamplight there came the sound of voices raised in heated debate and the sudden gust of laughter that suggested the wag was having his say.

They dismounted and tied up at the rail, stepped on to the plankwalk to kick mud from their boots. That done, Owen looked at Buck, at Tom, quietly said, 'No gunplay,' then boldly pushed through the swing doors into the glare of lamplight.

At once it was as if a blanket of thick velvet had descended on the room, muffling all sound. Flanked by his brothers, the three of them stock still with shock rocking them back on their heels,

144

Owen swept the room with eyes that revealed the enormity, the impossibility, of what they were trying to do. In that moment another terrible mistake was staring him in the face, disaster the only outcome. Fierce stares were directed on him from all sides. The room bristled with weapons, and hard hands reached for triggers as the silence was broken by a growing murmur of anger. He saw Kimball and Folsom, steely-eyed, their backs to the bar; men at tables, men to either side of the door so there could be no way out; Flanagan, in shirt sleeves dispensing drinks, the shotgun close to hand; Warren, with dark hair plastered by the rain and a face livid with anger. . . .

And Adam. Adam, flanked by two unshaven, bleary-eyed men. Adam – with a fierce, swashbuckling glint in his tired eyes.

'Your timing was right,' Owen said softly.

'Pure luck.'

'You bring the money?'

'Here, now?' Adam laughed out loud. 'What do you think?'

'Never mind what he thinks,' Frank Warren said, and he distanced himself from his drunken mob and stepped forward to confront Owen.

'Leave him be!' Nat Kimball snapped.

'Goddammit, Nat, these men robbed my bank, shot my daughter.'

'And now we've got a proposition to consider.'

'To hell with propositions. The money is town money, these men are thieves.'

'Then let's give the town back its money,' Owen said, 'and let the thieves go back to being simple ranchers.'

'The hell I will!'

'So, what then?' Kimball said, hands on hips, eyes cold. 'That money's hid, Warren. You hang four men, you become a thief yourself, deprive your fellow citizens of hard-earned cash they deposited in your bank for safe keeping.'

'Cash these men stole!' Warren roared.

'But cash that you have it in your power to recover, if you can swallow stupid pride.'

'I'll get it back, and still make them pay.' Warren's lips were flecked with spittle, his grin cruel. 'If you want a proposal to consider, how about this: we take them out of town, let three of them watch while we put a rope around the kid's neck and kick away his horse. You think they won't spill the beans, tell us where that gunny-sack's stashed, with the kid's face turning purple, his eyes bulging out of his head?'

When he leered at Owen, in a room suddenly stilled, there was triumph raging in his black eyes.

'All right, Mr Bank Robber, let's hear the smart reply.'

Chapter Eighteen

'I had you figured wrong,' Owen said.

'Damn right you did.'

'I reassured your woman, told her you were hard pressed, maybe bluffing. Told her you would have pulled back, got the men to douse those flaming torches if it looked like she was about to die.'

'I never bluff,' Warren said.

'Right. You don't look like a man who would even consider it,' Owen went on placidly. 'So I know you mean what you say about putting a rope around Buck's neck as a way of getting to that gunny-sack – and I can't figure out how you can be so goddamn stupid.'

A soft sigh whispered around the room. Somewhere a man coughed. A crooked grin flickered around Nat Kimball's lips.

But now Warren had moved up so close that his

belly was hard against Owen's belt buckle, his purple face and jutting chin thrust forward so that Owen could smell the sourness of his breath. A nerve twitched at the corner of his mouth; his big hands were balled into white-knuckled fists.

'What the hell do you mean, stupid?' he said hoarsely, chewing each word and spitting it wetly into Owen's face. 'You think I won't hang that kid? Or what? You think I don't understand men well enough to know you'll snap like a dry twig when you see the kid choking at the end of a rope?'

'What I think,' Owen said, 'is when you know where the money's stashed you have it in your mind to hang all four of us – and once we understand that, your threat becomes as empty as your bank's safe.'

He planted his hand on Warren's chest, tried to push him away. But the man was immovable, a solid rock that was as one with the earth. He took Owen's muscular shove, found it wanting and leaned into it. Then he sneered, and as he did so his balled fist came up in a roundhouse swing and exploded at the angle of Owen's jaw.

Owen was flung backwards as if hit by a train. His arms flailed helplessly. There was a muffled roaring in his ears, and a searing flash of light left his vision masked by a flickering red haze. He slammed into Buck, heard the kid's yell of outrage like a disembodied voice calling from a distant

148

cave. Then, with bones turned to jelly and muscles to water he hit the floor with his shoulders and the back of his head cracked sickeningly against the hard wet dirt.

He moaned, shook his head, rolled desperately away expecting the banker's boots to crash into his ribs with bone-cracking thuds. Instead there was a sudden, violent commotion, and above the roaring in his ears he caught the muted roar of voices. He got his arms under him, gathered his strength, pushed, and with a mighty effort made it to his knees. The roaring remained – and it was accompanied by the tinkling of a piano. Owen shook his head again, climbed shakily to his feet and, as he blinked owlishly through the haze, he realized that the banker's punch had broken the deadlock and the saloon had erupted.

Blood was coppery in his mouth. He spat, felt for his pistol, then took another slugging blow in the face from an unshaven man with a rifle in one hand who leaped at him with eyes blazing. This time he rolled with the punch, used the instinctive twisting reaction to bring his fist around in a left hook that took the man in the ear and sent him crashing full length across a table.

Lamplight was cutting through the haze across his eyes like sunlight through morning mist. Owen kicked bits of the splintered table out of the way, staggered back against the wall on wobbly legs and dragged a sleeve across his mouth as he squinted at the room that had become a raging battleground.

Tom was backed up against a battered old piano, shirt ripped from his shoulders, rocking musically on the yellowed keys as a man slugged at his unprotected belly. Adam was against the bar, held fast by red-bearded Flanagan's big hands that were clamped on his upper arms while a man hammered short punches that rocked Adam's head. Buck was fighting like a young wildcat. He kicked one man in the groin, used a hard backhand fist to bring blood spraying from another man's smashed nose, a jolting uppercut to fell a third, spitting shattered teeth.

In the centre of the room, Nat Kimball had Warren's shirt front bunched in his fist and, incredibly, was one-handedly pushing him back and lifting the heavy banker on to his toes. The marshal's eyes were steely as he snarled words that were lost in the din. As Owen watched, Warren shook his head violently, tore loose from Kimball's fist and stabbed a hand for his pistol.

Tom's face was now a greenish white. He began to slide off the piano. Owen came away from the wall in a rush, took a knee in the belly and an elbow in the face and grunted in agony. Then, through streaming eyes, he saw Buck spring from nowhere, hook his arm around the man hammering blows at Tom and hurl him to the floor.

A shotgun roared.

The second barrel blasted and dust showered from the roof.

The noise was cut as if by a knife.

Owen flicked a glance towards the banker.

Frank Warren was frozen, open-mouthed, his six-gun in his hand. In front of him, Nat Kimball was bent over with both hands clutching his face. Blood was seeping through his fingers.

Beyond them, on the bar, tendrils of smoke curled from Flanagan's shotgun barrel. Flanagan himself was draped face-down over the counter, his scalp streaming blood. Adam had slipped down the rough boards fronting the bar and was gazing about him groggily.

'Quit, right now!' Jim Folsom roared. 'The next man throws a punch winds up in the hoosegow.'

He was tall and straight behind the bar. His hand still rested on Flanagan's shotgun, but the pistol that had felled the saloonist was in his right fist, and the look in his eyes was savage.

'You, Frank, you're headed there anyways. Goddammit, I saw you pistol-whip Nat—'

'Leave it, Jim,' Kimball said. He cuffed the banker out of the way, dragged off his bandanna and dabbed at the blood pouring from his slashed cheekbone. Then he swung on Warren.

'All right, now this is the way we handle it—'

'Now you listen here—'

'Just shut your goddamm mouth, Frank. You've waived any rights to a say in this.'

'Jesus, Kimball, if you let them get away with this—'

'No winners, no losers. In a couple of hours we'll all be older and wiser, but apart from wounds that'll take time to heal it'll be like nothing ever happened. The cash'll be back in your safe. These four fellers will be someplace else.'

'That's the aim,' Warren said, tight lipped. 'What about the workings of it? When we get to where it's hidden, how can you be sure these fellers will hand over that gunny-sack?'

'Yeah, and how can I be sure him and his cronies won't take the cash, then hang us all?' Owen said, and looked enquiringly at Kimball.

The marshal dabbed at his cheek, swore softly.

'Because this is between you and me,' he said tightly.

Buck was watching Owen. Adam was hanging on to the bar, carefully waggling his battered jaw from side to side. The piano emitted a ghostly tinkle as Tom eased himself upright.

'And my brothers,' Owen said quietly, and Kimball nodded.

'You hand the cash to me, you're all free to go.'

They were a mile out of town, riding across the flooded plain in the growing light of dawn with

Adam in the lead when Nat Kimball said, 'I figured free booze and Jim Folsom with a shotgun was enough to hold 'em. I figured wrong.'

'There's only one way to stop a man like that,' Owen said.

'Not easy,' Kimball said. 'I count eight of 'em followin' us, plus Warren.'

'Too many,' Owen said grimly.

Adam looked over his shoulder and laughed. 'Depends on the quality, and who they're up against.'

'I'll grant you they're roostered,' Kimball called, 'but all the red-eye in the West don't stop a man pullin' the trigger.'

They rode through the patchy rain in silence, Owen intermittently glancing over his shoulder to see Warren and his men keeping station a few hundred yards back. He had already guessed where Adam had stashed the bank's cash, and knew that Warren would have looked ahead and reached the same conclusion.

The boulder from which the town had taken its name was a brooding edifice against the lightening skies, the boughs of the pines on its crest hanging dark and limp in the now still air.

As they rode up the final long slope and turned on to the expanse of buffalo grass leading to the cliff face, the shallow cave, Owen recalled their wild night ride through the storm, the fierce argument in the lee of the big rock; the way he and Adam had reached agreement of a sort and swapped hats in the rain.

That was when, together, they had fashioned hope out of dark disaster, picked themselves up by the bootstraps after the low point reached with the bungled bank robbery and the sight of Tom going down to Nat Kimball's bullet, Buck pinned beneath his horse with a rifle muzzle at his head. From there they had gone forward, Adam to news of Ike down in Austin that was half expected, Owen to a fouled-up jail-break that had come right through Tom's bravery.

And now Adam again. Together they had planned the return of the money if the need for it was spirited away by a hangman's noose. Adam had found the guts to ride back into Boulder Halt. But still, Owen acknowledged, it might not have worked without Nat Kimball's help; still might not be pulled off, for nine to four odds were awesome, and who could say which way Kimball would swing once the bank's stolen money was safe in his hands?

But even as he allowed himself the bitter-sweet comfort of those thoughts, the drum of hooves coming up fast from behind told him that Frank Warren was taking no chances.

'Go ahead,' Kimball said tightly. 'I'll hold them. I figure you put the cash in that cave. Dig out that gunny-sack, put it on the ground in the open where I can see it.'

'It could be empty.'

Kimball grinned and shook his head.

'You ain't got the brains, Lawson.'

Owen and Kimball were fifty yards from the bluff when the marshal reined in, the others that far ahead, Adam already swinging from the saddle. Owen reached them in a rush as Adam emerged from the cave dragging the damp, earth-smeared gunny-sack.

'Out in the open, on the ground,' Owen said. 'Hold it high, first, so Kimball can see.'

'Kimball's finished,' Buck said with panic in his voice.

'Jesus!' Owen said, and watched the nine men swallow up the marshal, saw his horse go down, heard the vicious crack of the shot.

Then Warren was coming for them. He rode at the head of his lynch-mob, a burly figure riding tall in the saddle, the pistol glinting in his big fist ominous yet insignificant among the weapons bristling all around him.

'Let them come,' Adam said.

'What!'

'They're wasting their time.'

'How the hell can you say—'

'I guess there's something about this place,' Adam said with maddening calm.

'Yeah,' Owen said, 'it's beginning to look awful like some places I know they call boot hill.'

'What I mean is, every time we come here, we argue – and that reminds me, you're wearin' my hat.'

'Owen,' Buck said shakily, his eyes on the approaching horsemen, 'what in hell do we do?'

'We ride out of here, nice and easy,' Adam said placidly.

'And get shot in the back?'

'It won't happen.'

With a last, uncomprehending look into his brother's eyes, Owen pulled his horse around, turned his back on the lynch-mob and rode away from the bluff. He heard Buck's gasp of horror, heard the jingle of bridles, the swish of hooves through wet leaves. Then they had caught up with him. In line abreast, they rode away from Frank Warren and his cronies at a trot, and the skin on Owen's back crawled as Warren's roar of rage was followed by the crackle of pistols.

Then, from high overhead, a rifle cracked.

Another heavier long gun boomed from the trees away to their right.

'What the hell!'

Adam grinned happily. 'Four owlhoot pards, you said. Waitin' in Austin to bust Ike out of jail.'

'That's them?' Owen said, swinging in the saddle to look towards the two men who had

156

ridden out of the trees; turning again to peer upwards to the tall pines on the bluff where two dark figures were now crouched. 'You knew this would happen, all along – because they rode up the line with you?'

'With Ike dead, there was nothing for them in Austin. They're headin' for Hole in The Wall. I told them I could use their firepower, so they rode after me at their own pace.'

'They've stopped!' Buck cried. 'Warren's turnin' back – and Kimball's on his feet!'

'Hellfire,' Owen roared. 'It's over!'

It was – and they knew it.

Buck went first, howling and flapping his hat. He was followed by Tom, askew in the saddle as he favoured his bruised ribs, but laughing out loud. Adam was close behind – but first he took a moment to wave acknowledgement to the four men with rifles who were coming together at the foot of the bluff to head north-west.

Then Owen gleefully put spurs to his mount. He rode through his brothers like the wind, and then he was up in his stirrups crazily yelling.

'So where are we heading for, lads?'

Back came the delighted chorus.

'North a ways.'

'Are we ever comin' back to Boulder Halt?'

And as the cries of, 'No, feller, we ain't *never* comin' back,' rang out over the prairie, the clouds broke overhead and, through a shaft of brilliant sunlight, the Lawson boys headed for home.